Tattle Tales:
Essays and Stories Along the Way
Abbe Rolnick
First Edition
Copyright © 2016 Abbe Rolnick

Sedro Publishing
21993 Grip Road
Sedro Woolley, WA 98284
www.sedropublishing.com

Library of Congress Control Number: 2016908318
ISBN 978-0-9845119-5-2 (trade book)
ISBN 978-0-9845119-6-9 (electronic book)
Cover design and prepress by Karen Parker (www.karenparkerdesigns.com)

Editorial Assistance: Sara Stamey (www.sarastamey.com)

Other books by Abbe Rolnick
River of Angels (2010) *Color of Lies* (2013) *Cocoon of Cancer: An Invitation to Love Deeply* (2016)

Tattle Tales:
Essays and Stories Along the Way

Abbe Rolnick

Sedro
Publishing

GARY —
Enjoy the Tales
Abbe

TABLE OF CONTENTS

Prologue

In this collection, *Tattle Tales: Essays and Stories Along the Way*, I have blurred the lines of nonfiction and fiction, truth and imagination. I ask the reader to believe in each "tattle" as a part of a larger view on life. Truth has many layers, viewpoints give a perspective, slices create a feel, and putting them together, the reader sees more of the author, more of themselves, and can enter other worlds.

I've arranged the "tattles" thematically in stages of life: seeker, childhood moments, maturing, a-musing, and traveler. Humor, discovery, observation, life lessons, and imagination are interspersed within each telling.

Take my "tattle tales" off the bookshelf (who knows where they will be filed) and enjoy.

Seeking

Joy

I begin this collection with the thought I place before my closed eyes as I end my day and ponder, "What joy did I receive?" and as I rise I ask myself, "What joy will I bring to others?"

Having passed the half century mark, I'd like to believe that I'm wiser and funnier than when I was younger, that I know what the world is about. What I've found is that my years of maturing have brought me one simple gem to believe in. I've put aside politics, religion, and any structure that defines too specifically the nature of life. I simply believe in joy.

Joy is not synonymous with happiness. Happiness comes and goes, fleeting with the acquisition or failure of things based on needs, wants, or achievements. Joy is less transitory, less vulnerable. I liken the difference between joy and happiness to the Spanish words, *feliz* and *contento*. The word *feliz* is accompanied by the verb *ser*, which means a state of being. *Contento* uses the verb *estar*, to be, but it is only how you are for that one brief moment.

Joy runs deeper than happiness. It includes the shades of darkness that balance and contrast the light. Joy reveals the unknown, the unexpected parts we'd like to forget or ignore. It has more to do with listening than attaining, feeling and understanding rather than fixing. To be joyful in the darkness is to accept life in its entirety. Living with joy is to discover the freedom of letting go of perceptions and receiving what is present. Joy is a choice to accept the unexpected, to acknowledge all that passes one's way. Joy is to feel connected even at the prospect of loss.

Joy is to love despite the risk of rejection, recognizing that love is an honor not to be discarded. Joy comes from the tasting of flavors, intensity, and gentle forms of love. Acceptance with grace transforms love outside the realm of the purely physical. It encompasses the gradations, the use of all our senses. To be joyful, one embraces the essence of another person in a hug, wraps oneself around the ideas swarming in another's head. Joy communicates through a willingness to share, by opening up and revealing regardless of the outcome.

Joy lies beneath the stone that blocks your path. It is found behind the door of fear that stops you from feeling or attempting something new. Joy is curious, precocious, and forgiving. Joy is your playmate, up for the adventure, affectionately bestowing kindness and prodding you along, exposing and protecting you all at the same time. Joy is a process that encompasses all of life. It is being alive.

I believe that living with joy in my heart creates the wisdom and laughter that will sustain me for another half century.

Lace

Written during a time of transition, this story melds elements of my fascination with ocean creatures, other cultures, youthful naivety, and the lessons of becoming new.

The cramped four-seater biplane circled for a landing. Rose searched the aqua-blue waters below, trying to pinpoint their ultimate destination. Coral atolls, orange starfish, and silver-white flashes sparkled through the crystal clear water. She wondered if they were going to use the pontoons for a landing as they hovered close to a lagoon. But the pilot turned the nose of the plane upward again. On the third pass, Rose realized that at the top of the small mountain peak a flat brown section completely stripped of vegetation served as the runway.

The guidebook had stated, "Come to our island peak for your Caribbean holiday. Secluded, remote adventures you won't forget." The description was accurate. She had assumed that the island would be larger, more like her own that stretched out its presence across the equatorial Atlantic waters for ninety miles. Compared to the crowded Latino shores of Puerto Rico, this island was merely a postage stamp coming to a point. But size hadn't been a prerequisite for adventure and solitude.

Rose mumbled praise and thanks to any of the gods who would listen, "Beautiful skies, nice weather, tiny plane, let me down gently." She peered through the pilot's window, lost faith, sealed her eyes closed, and held her breath. At the last minute she took courage and peeled her lids open in time to see houses rising along mountainsides – almost touching the wings. Sun rays bounced back from tin roofs, and a rainbow of colors reflected off the chrome of the plane. She saw the world through colored bubbles, a series of looped holes. The plane twisted and veered sideways as the runway met its tires. Rose felt the thump and screech of rubber and then the silence of being down.

As the only passenger, she stepped off immediately. A small beat-up Jeep pulled alongside the plane. A richly tanned man leaned his head out the window. "I say, do you need a ride?" His British accent seemed too sweet, almost a solicitation.

She waved him on. "No, my feet need stretching." More importantly, her heart needed time. Rose raised her head toward the sun, determined to make her own way, be independent. Seven years of faithfulness in a failed marriage had left her with a hole where caring used to be.

"Are you sure, Miss? The hotel is pretty far from here."

"Yes, I'm quite sure."

Rose lifted her backpack onto her shoulders and began the trek up and down and around the meandering mountain. Occasionally she'd stop to rest, only to see the beater of a car following behind. She'd walk, the car would follow, she'd stop, and the car would halt. Each time Rose smiled and waved. She had the road to herself, except for a few mules loaded with wares and their owners who acknowledged her presence with a nod or a half wave. Small houses lay scattered along the hillside. Up higher, white stucco mansions overlooked the road. More than an hour passed before she finally arrived at a group of colonial, whitewashed cottages that bore the name Island Resort. Just after the divorce had become final she'd reserved one of these cottages for the week, one day for each year of marriage, as a promise to herself of a future.

Dressed in tropical holiday fare—sandals, short shorts, sundresses—and the more formal khakis with plaid short-sleeved shirts—guests milled around the open-air lobby. Compared with the Spanish flair of bright pastel colors, gaudy paintings, and wood carvings, the decoration of the main lodge felt stuffy, plain, and judgmental. Red overstuffed chairs sat in formation on the shiny white-tiled floor, and somber paintings adorned the walls. The guide book Rose had used warned the tourist to look beyond the snobbish attitude of the British. The porter at the desk looked amused, not snobbish. He laughed when he saw her. "Hello, Miss Rose. Did you enjoy your walk?"

She was about to ask how he knew her name, but by then more locals from the town had appeared. They chuckled and smiled, peering expectantly at her.

Rose's embarrassment crept along her neck to her cheeks and covered her face. She'd been so caught up in wanting to be strong and fearless that she didn't see the obvious. Red-faced, Rose recognized the Jeep driver. "Why didn't you tell me?"

He shrugged. "You didn't ask."

A tall, lean woman with closely-cropped grey hair and wire-rimmed glasses, dressed in a pale lemon linen suit, escorted Rose to her cottage. She painstakingly showed her the bathroom, tapping on the walls as she turned on the water. The pipes creaked and sputtered. The hot water ran cold, then rusty red, then boiling hot. She warned her that they lost the water altogether later in the day. As an early riser, Rose had the best chance of getting hot water. A note stated that breakfast would be left at the door between 7:00 and 8:00 am, and she was to choose her meal. Rose marked fruit and a muffin and a 7:00 am delivery, unpacked her bag, and made her way down to the harbor.

For an island this small, the harbor impressed her with a wharf made of stone extending along the shoreline and allowing for two piers. One of the piers, designated for the local fishermen, secured a dozen small wooden rowboats filled with freshly caught flat, silvery flounder. Although Rose felt a sense of connection with the fishermen, she headed to the second pier that housed the luxury yachts.

In planning her healing adventure months before, she had researched the scuba situation and booked a dive for the late afternoon. Through a series of third-party phone calls and letters and picture swapping, Rose was given the name and description of her guide. She had sent her modest diving statistics along, anticipating the rigors of remote dives in open, dangerous waters. It wasn't difficult to spot where she was to go. Standing on a large sailboat marked Island Divers stood a tall, muscular, tanned figure dressed in what looked like five inches of a stretched brown rubber band. Every glossy ripple of skin marked him the diver.

As Rose stepped on board, Randy nodded her way and told her to stow her gear. She offered her hand as an introduction. Four brown fingers and a half thumb clasped Rose's ringless hand. Heat encircled her palm, brushing her with an electric wave of burning need. She couldn't tell from which direction the charge came. "You must be Randy. I'm Rose."

He released her hand and nodded. "I know. The town watched your grand arrival hours ago."

Dismissed, Rose covered her embarrassment by following his gaze as he watched a large yacht docking two slips down from his sailboat. He turned, looked her up and down, and said, "How long does your tank last?"

She thought back to all her previous dives, the ones in storms or caves, and the easy free-floating ones. "They last forever. I usually come back with at least a half a tank."

He took that information in. "Are you good with strangers?"

Randy was a stranger. She didn't think he meant that. "I run a bookstore and deal with the public, if that is your question."

Randy looked her in the eyes for the first time. He smiled, and she noticed that his shoulders began to relax. "Good, then you can help me on this dive. My assistant didn't show. The letter you sent with your statistics, if they're true, means you can dive in difficult situations. Just by looking at your physique, I know you can help. I have fifteen scuba divers from New England arriving on that cruise ship. They think they know how to dive, and will bring all sorts of fancy gear. It will be your job to read their regulators and tell me when they are running out of air."

She didn't have time to agree or disagree. The change in the terms of their agreement wasn't a question, more of an expectation. At least someone expected something of her.

Fifteen tourists approached the sailboat. They all had large duffle bags and looked serious. Randy introduced her as his assistant. She checked everyone's gear, appreciating the new title and role. Two engineers showed her their deluxe watches and depth gauges. They all had wetsuits.

They set out sailing toward a secluded reef about a half hour from the island. The boat glided through aqua-green, crystal clear, smooth water. Rose listened to heroic exploits as the sun reflected the blue sky and waters back and forth. Although she had never been to this spot before, the smells of salt and fish, the striking sense of purity, of colors focused, and the sunbaked heat were reminiscent of her previous life. But all of that life had been chaffed away. Rose stood exposed, trying to absorb the beauty and simplicity through her skin, to rekindle her heart and see beyond the holes. Healing takes time. She stood on the deck of the boat, anonymous to herself.

Randy focused on the logistics of the dive, leaving Rose to make small talk and put the divers at ease. They were to be down at an easy depth of thirty-two feet for about an hour. Randy sent her over first. Dressed in only her swimsuit, fins, mask, tank and regulator, with the simplest of watches and gauges, she did a backward roll over the side of the boat and headed downward. Rose waited, counting until all fifteen divers were down. Randy came last.

They used the buddy system, with Randy at the lead. The numbers were odd, so she floated back and forth with various partners, all the while checking everyone's regulators. Rose didn't register many of the fish or sites, as she was too busy watching the engineers. Their air depleted too quickly. She finally motioned a thumb-up sign to Randy, signaling that they needed to return. After only half an hour, their tanks showed only ten minutes left of air. She led them back to the surface and helped them back into the boat. The rest of the group came with Randy, feeling elated and superior.

Randy and Rose barely talked. The tourists left, and they cleaned up. She'd been on many dives before and knew the protocol on removing sand and salt from all the gear. She didn't mind the work, but needed some sign from Randy to validate her worth.

As Rose left, he looked at her tank and noticed that the tank was almost full of air. "You don't use much air, do you? You'd be good on my deep dives where I hunt for black jewels."

Rose was tired, and wondered what he was planning. She couldn't tell if he was offering her a job or a compliment. When she didn't respond, he placed his brown hands on her shoulders and tilted her head up to look at his eyes. "Hey, I apologize for today. Your dive will be with just me tomorrow. No charge."

"I wasn't worried about the money. I just need to be underwater."

"Well, then I'll see you tomorrow about eleven."

∞

The vibrant orange of the Flamboyant flower and perfume of fresh white orchids greeted her. The vase took center stage on the lone table, filling the room with smells of comfort and welcome. She showered and sang, "*Que sera, sera*. Whatever will be, will be." She put on a backless sundress handmade for her by her dearest lady friend for occasions of celebration. Rose had nothing to celebrate yet, only the anticipation of a few afternoons and evenings filled with possibilities. Leaving the door closed but unlocked, she headed into the market.

A cobblestone road led her to an area packed with booths and tables. Tourists in their Bermuda shorts with cameras dangling peered at the merchandise. Absent were fruit vendors, books, hardware, and shaved ice, the essentials that she would have found at the heart of her own island. She walked slowly, examining pottery, wood carvings, and lace. All the crafts appealed to the senses, made with natural woods or dyed the color of fruits, but one bent, white-haired lady's lace kept drawing her back. The fine, intricate stitches looped one on top of the other, leaving few visible holes, giving a sense of completeness, a wholeness she craved. The complicated pattern told a story. Rose studied the tablecloth and saw the surrounding village populated by mountains, trees, and the ocean. There were fisherman with nets, women hanging clothes, and children playing in the streets. Rose had to have the tablecloth. It reminded her of one made by her grandmother, whose lacework held the traditions of her life growing up in Russia. This one resembled that of the island she lived on, the warmth she used to feel, that she would soon be leaving.

The old lady smiled a toothless smile at her when she asked to purchase the lace. The price was outrageous at $75 in US currency. They dickered for a while, and Rose finally gave in at $60.

"I will wrap it nicely for you and mail it to your home."

"I'd prefer to take it with me now."

"I must finish the stitching around the edges. I will mail it to you."

The smiles from the old lady didn't falter, but Rose did. Reluctantly she gave her the address and money. She had no card, but assured Rose how happy she'd be when the cloth arrived. She would even send her four lace napkins for free.

Rose walked off, wanting desperately to believe in her, but not so sure of any of the guarantees.

∞

Dinner at the hotel was formal. The insistence of tea and the multi-layered place settings gave it a British feel. She arrived late, still wearing her backless sundress. She felt exposed, too vulnerable, wanting to cover her shoulders, cover her heart. She tried to make small talk, but all her skills at making strangers feel comfortable had been drained by the tourists from New England.

Unsettled by the dinner, Rose was not ready to turn in and be alone in her bed. Nights were harder to face after the divorce. The arguments, hurts, and fears would lie alongside her, keeping her from sleep, keeping her from healing. She had traveled thousands of miles from her home hoping to escape the pain, but it had come along. She drank a tropical blitz and then another. She felt giddy, and as she walked outside she heard drum beats, rhythmic music played to the pounding ocean. She sat staring out at the stars. Almost all the tourists had retired, but still she sat alone with her thoughts. In the corner where the local band played, Rose spied Randy. Local women in long, flowing bright skirts swayed with the music, surrounded him in swirls of color. He said nothing, but drank with his shoulders hunched, occasionally looking in her direction.

Rose made no move toward him, but she knew he had seen her. When he was ready to leave, he walked over to her and took her hand. She felt his stubby thumb and took comfort in its misshapen form. They walked out to his car. In the parking lot, two of Randy's diver friends passed around a bottle of rum to share. Rose without thinking took a swig, and all four of them hopped into Randy's car. An air of need permeated the car. Wordlessly the four of them listened to the wind and ocean. Transformed in a stupor of swells and pulses, with a hint of alcohol, Rose absorbed the waves. They drove back to Randy's house guided by the moon along the winding road that paralleled the shore. Rose thought the inevitable hook-up with Randy would happen, but something else did instead.

Rose never knew Randy's friends' names, but they knew hers. At his house, Randy disappeared, and with his absence came their separate embraces. A moment of panic ensued as the lights went out and the door slammed. Rose closed her eyes, tried to visualize the road back to her cottage. Dizzy with alcohol, she pushed and pulled her body to go nowhere. They called out her name over and over. Their cries were of passion and longing and what felt like caring. Rose was the object of their fantasy. She sealed herself in an invisible bubble and vanished. Her body might have responded to them, but Rose kept her thoughts and emotions separate. She had sought the promise of strength, tanned muscles, warmth, passion, and mutual adventure. But Randy's arms never held her. He returned, but remained stiff and withdrawn. His body was for show, his heart emptier than hers.

∞

Rose dressed in the wee hours of the morning and started the long walk back to her cottage. She noticed the sun rising over the water, could see the reflections of color making the day new. Her body was a shell holding a heart filled with terror, grief, and lost love. The road's surface was bumpy. The soles of her sandals grabbed the bumps so that each step fell into an awkward cadence. Rose got a sick pleasure out of the roughness of the spaces between the smooth stones. Each jagged spot poked at her feet. She imagined all the people who had walked down this same road to create the glossy, even stones. Eventually the pattern between rough and smooth would wear itself out so that someone other than her could experience that sameness. There was no smoothness in Rose's life now. The gnawing emptiness was pointed, sharp, jabbing at her heart. Yet Rose had once been capable of soothing, being the smooth surface that appeases others' pain. She had embraced her marriage with joy, passion, and caring, but somehow she had veiled herself, refusing to see the holes in their cover.

Rose smelled the beginning of morning wafting from the houses along the hillside. Light blossomed in a cluttered kitchen displaying fresh papaya, grapefruit, and handpicked eggs scrambled, still moist, alongside homemade bread. It could have been her house, only her kitchen was now empty. Waiting at her cottage doorstep was a breakfast of warm muffins, fruit, and tea. Grateful as she was, Rose was too depleted to eat. She sat alone, sipping the proper English tea, and closed her eyes.

∞

At eleven she walked down to the harbor. Randy stood like a Greek statue on his boat. He had already checked her gear and refilled the tank. No one came with them except the strong wind. They sailed a good half hour out to an area where Randy said few divers go. They didn't talk about themselves. They didn't need to. Rose no longer saw Randy's muscles or tan. His skimpy swimsuit was not worn for her benefit. His body was hard, his hands callused from hard work and abuse. He sought punishment and salvation for untold sins of love he wanted to commit. He was a man without a heart made for love.

Randy went over the routine they'd follow once in the water. If Rose was fearful or had a problem, she was to tug on the rope attached between them. Rose rolled off the side of the boat first. Immediately she was encircled by baby silver sharks. She counted twenty and then swam deeper, as Randy had advised. The dive sparkled, shimmered her back into life. Beautiful fairy basslets, schools of yellow and blue grunt, black and white angelfish hid along with the gnarly puffers and rocky scorpionfish amongst the red fire-coral. Randy took the lead into a cave. Only their headlamps gave light to the darkness. Tethered to him by the rope,

Rose trusted in Randy's abilities, his knowledge of the underwater world. She'd seen the ocean's bottom before, but the juxtaposition of the beauty and danger had never affected her so deeply. Life was so full of perils that were beyond her control, yet she could coexist, flirt with risk and remain intact.

Randy behaved like a dolphin swimming above and below her, always in sight. Neither of them tugged on the rope. They came up after an hour of exploring. They worked well together. They sailed back, talking only of what they'd seen. There were silences, but they held no promises. Their thoughts were separate, carrying only the truth of what they observed. Randy looked at her regulator to see how much air she had used. His tank was almost on empty, but Rose still had half a tank. As she said goodbye, Randy called out, "You'd make a good jewel diver. The pay is good, but the work is illegal."

∞

That night Rose mingled with the guests, able to socialize and listen to their stories. The New England divers were long gone, safe in their yacht. At her table sat well-dressed men and women. They were seasoned visitors, returning year after year. She laughed with them as they tried to impress her with their successes, but Rose could see that they were all really the same, searching for the one thing that would bring them true contentment.

Over the next two days, she meandered through the hills, taking trails up into old overgrown neighborhoods where homes had been abandoned and left to nature. Behind security fences of old electrical wire lay lives covered with weeds gone wild. She found one spot where a small rock garden had retained its shape. Sweet Williams, pink, red, and white, waved to her in the wind. Rose had found her happiness for the day.

On the morning she was due to return, her British driver was waiting at the cottage. Rose got into his beater of a car and headed up and down the mountain until they reached the narrow road the islanders called a runway. The driver beamed the entire way, telling stories of the locals—who lived where, who cheated on their wives, and how much he loved his job.

Again, she was the only passenger on the plane. The pilot skipped the safety instructions, but offered a small prayer in its place. They accelerated and within seconds lifted off the peak to circle the small cone of an island. Rose spotted Randy's boat and what she believed to be the coral reef they had explored. Three plane rides later, she touched down on her old island home.

It took her a week to back her belongings, but Rose waited four more weeks for the lace tablecloth that never arrived. She exhaled completely, and moved on.

Snow Darts

The white of snow—innocence—and the treacherous road through business and love intermingle as a young adult tries to find moral ground.

The rain abruptly changes to thick, hard pellets. It's as if I've crossed some major divide, a splitting off into the worlds of moral principles. The rainy side with fog and poor visibility shrouds the meek questioners, those incapable of and refusing to make any decision. The slippery side, covered in white, leads to a path lined in ice. On this side, principles slide across an imaginary line, hard and slick. Any action taken on thin ice leaves me cold.

My hands clutch the steering wheel in a death grip. My head throbs. Driving is a necessity, the only way home. For a while I can see through the blinding snowflakes, looking through the stream of white blowing into my face. I follow the tracks ahead of me, just as I have done at work. The stories of controversial contracts, employees with questionable ethics, injustice of ethnic inequality, all create a path established before my entrance as the boss. The road to change, what I call progress, will come with slow, steady steps.

The snow comes down, swirling all around, and my view to either side is obscured. I don't dare look behind me, but I sense by the light in my mirror that a semi-truck hugs my tail. I pray that I won't have to slam on my brakes and feel the past come ramming through my window.

In my position, I am accountable for all decisions, past and present. The excuse that I didn't know holds no weight. So I open Pandora's Box and rifle through, sorting, fixing, and changing. My stomach knots at what I find, the unraveling painful. The road I am on is familiar, but I can't see stop signs or traffic lights. I worry that I won't be able to stop without swerving off the road. I downshift and ease through the intersection. I hold my breath as the snow comes straight at me.

The storm is not friendly. Each snowflake takes the shape of an arrow, swirling at all angles like snow darts trying to break through the windshield. Suddenly I am very hot. I want to open the windows, let some air in, perhaps escape. I see myself cornered in an office. The explosion of words and anger in my face sends off alarms. I can only remain seated with no exit. I wait until the anger subsides. I try re-explaining, looking for a way to criticize and elicit a change. My futile attempts hit the wall of expectations. Asking an employee to change after years of being left to poor habits seems like an invasion of territory. To his view, I am insane. All that counts in his view is profitability. Accountability, respect, regulations are not in the scope of his job description. I am alone in my request and alone in my defense.

I know where I am, not by what I see around me. I can feel the rise in the road, sense by the speed of my car that I am on the last hill before my road. I know inside what is right. Bullying creates a deep sadness inside. I want to stop the car, have someone rescue me from any sort of responsibility. But I fire the bully and bear the brunt of his vicious accusations. I feel the snow darts hit their target. My heart deflates as I pull up to my home. A chill runs up my spine and along my arms. Surrounded by snow, my house forms a large white mound of innocence. I am surprised at the crackle of lightning and the roll of thunder. The storm is confused, trying to rain, but instead white light falls. I wonder at my principles and on what side of the road I live on.

Puzzled

History, politics, and the environment within the grass of a mowed lawn.

I am known to be honest to a fault, conservative with my money, and generous with my heart. I'd like to think of myself as responsible, but I'm not so sure that Abe Lincoln or Alexander Hamilton would concur. We have had a run-in today from across the centuries. I've symbolically destroyed the physical evidence of their political history.

Normally my thoughts aren't so complicated. I take that back, I'm simplistic with lots of complexities, but it doesn't always show. Today, as I tackle the long grass on my six-acre parcel, my mind is empty of thought. I take pride as I walk behind the mower. I've gotten the blade down low enough to crop the grass neatly but avoid the rocks. I've made a pact with myself to eliminate the grinding sound of metal and rock, the flying pieces of pebbles in the air, and the inevitable chips and bends that accompany my over-zealous need to have a clean cut.

I've discovered that if I loop around the house without turning up and down rows, the manicuring of the lawn is sexier. Mowing is like life. It is all about curves and swirls. The surprises are found in the turns, the forever greening of virgin grass with the new tips rising from the ground, grown wild with temptation. Circling the lawn in spirals and twirls is like peeling away all that is hidden to reveal the inner side; it feels like the peeling of an apple with its skin still intact. I mow with imperfect precision, no straight lines, no declared patterns. The loose tufts of greenery smile back at me as if they too know that life is messy.

I've always been fascinated with Abe Lincoln, the champion of slaves, a man who would walk a mile to give a customer the correct change. I've thought of him as a man for the underdog, a man who could understand my tendency to talk with strangers, experience other cultures, and put myself in other people's shoes. He would understand why I have trouble asking for help to fix the plumbing, or the noise in my steering wheel. He would understand why I curse in another language, falsely believing that if no one understands what I am saying, it can't be bad.

For some reason, as a child I believed that Abe Lincoln was a distant relative. I was supposed to be named Abraham, which was converted to Abbe when I arrived female instead of the expected male. No matter that my namesake was my grandfather, not the 16th President of the United States. I know more about Abe Lincoln than I do about my own grandfather, Abraham Javodick. There must be a secret that I'm not privy to, some hidden truth or embarrassment that no one wants to reveal. Perhaps for this reason, I've made Abe Lincoln my own. Sticking with the facts, I can avoid some personal messes. Even as I write this, I feel that I'm cheating. For I often ponder the picture of my grandfather with his hand resting on my grandmother's shoulder. Was his hand light and affectionate, or hard and demanding? The truth lies somewhere in the curve of his gnarled fingers, the circle not yet completed.

Not long ago the land I now mow was woods and swamp, or what is termed wetlands. My house sits on the only site allowed for development. The politics of a landowner have been complicated as history marches forth into the present. Landowners' rights no longer deal with slavery but the preservation of the environment. I follow the rules and make sure that I nurture the trees and keep my footprint small. I prune back the bramble of the blackberries, avoiding more wounds as their creeping branches brush along my bare arms and legs while I swirl around the grass. When the sun shines, I mow with as much skin visible as possible. Sun on skin is my antidote to emotional bruises. I seek deeper warmth that penetrates my skin to my heart and acts as a shield against the prickly thorns of life. Mother Nature rests her hand on my shoulder, warmly allowing me to bare more truth.

I confess that until today, I had paid little attention to the historical figure of Alexander Hamilton. He was never one of my early heroes. But given my negligence and wandering thoughts as I mowed, I found myself searching the internet to find his place in history. I discovered that without him we would have no National Bank or way to produce currency. As the first Secretary of the Treasury, he was responsible for the minting of the U.S. currency. He turned our world green by pulling all of the coins and currency from the various states into a uniform system. He alone is responsible for our treasury notes. Today we talk of green. By this we mean to live by preserving our natural resources, to live more honestly with little waste. Alexander Hamilton would know nothing of the "greening of America" in this sense. My true hero, Abe Lincoln, stopped the South from seceding from the Union. Alexander Hamilton drew the nation together with the establishment of the U.S. Treasury.

It is within this currency legacy that the worlds of Abraham Lincoln, Alexander Hamilton, and Abbe merge. On my last pass around the house, I scan the swirls of cut grass, admiring the remnants of curves and the tidiness of my lawn. To my dismay, I notice amongst the cuttings the number five and the number ten, pieces of money sliced by my mower. Under my breath I murmur, *Cojones fritas*, cursing in my non-native language. Somehow money from my pocket had fallen, and with one turn of the mower I have destroyed the face of Abe Lincoln on the five-dollar bill and the face of Alexander Hamilton on the ten-dollar bill.

The sun slips behind a cloud, and my bare arms and legs feel the goose bumps rise in salute. I bend down and collect as many pieces as I can find. Inside my house, I start sorting. I learn from the internet who adorned each of our treasury bills, where the serial numbers were placed, the monuments on each bill, and the placement of the words In God We Trust. I pass over an hour putting the bills back together. Gradually the ragged remnants weed themselves out until I have put the puzzle back together. The faces of Abe and Alex peer out at me.

Along the way I felt the gentle presence of Abe sitting on my shoulder. I heard him whisper that the politics of life change, that even though he was a Republican, he was a Democrat at heart. Alexander was more passionate with his whispering. He died in a duel defending his honor after having a love affair outside of his marriage, and his words were more judgmental. The irony of the ages.

Banks will exchange money that is at least fifty percent intact. Abe is now 75% whole, and Alexander 50%. Knowing this, I choose not to make the exchange. Instead, each bill remains on my refrigerator amongst pictures of my children, family friends, quotes of the day, and my dreams. Each bill is a visual reminder of the importance of history and that life is fragile and transitory. Putting the pieces back together presents another turn, another curve, a little more mess. I look at Abe and Alex daily, and they remind me that I have chosen to remain 100% me, with all my faults.

Childhood

The Silent War

A childhood memory of a carpenter sets the stage for understanding the horrors of the Holocaust.

I went to grade school during the *Cold War*. My understanding of the *Cold War* was tied to my desk. Whenever the subject would come up in school, we would have a practice air raid. Air raids resemble a fire drill, except that we never left the building. We would hide under our desks. I was lucky because I was small and could curl under without any part of my body being exposed. This made me feel extremely safe, and I knew I'd be warm. At home we also practiced for an air raid. My sister and I would hide in the back part of our basement. This is where my mother hung our laundry to dry. It was damp and dark, and toward the corner there was a hidden crawl space where my parents kept Spam, Campbell's Soup, water, chocolate, and crackers in a locked compartment. I never felt safe there, as spiders and bugs were frequent visitors and the dampness kept me shivering.

Our indoor play area was supposed to be in the basement. Not the back part where our raids were held, but in the newly paneled section. It was my mother's idea to make the basement cozier. She decorated the room in black and white checks with an accent of red. I took a keen interest in the redoing of the basement. The carpenter she hired to panel the walls was named Joseph. The first thing I noticed about him was his hair. It was the unruly type, which is different from unkempt. You could tell he had brushed it, but the curls popped up everywhere, despite his efforts. They curled down his neck and through the sleeves of his flannel shirt.

He always came to our house in the same outfit, burnt-orange coveralls worn over a flannel shirt. When he was warm, Joseph rolled up his shirtsleeves above his elbows. That was when I saw the blue numbers etched on his wrists.

When Joseph started working for us, my Mom told me not to make a pest of myself. She warned me that Joseph was moody; a good worker, but moody. No one bothered him except me. And I really don't think he considered me a bother. At first Joseph didn't talk. I would come down the stairs, find a place amongst the ladders and tools, and watch. He would look at me, his eyes large and blue, hooded by curly eyebrows. We'd stare at one another until I could detect a small nod, which I interpreted as a signal of welcoming. I would plop myself down, waiting to be needed. Gradually I could tell when he needed his hammer or nails. I became his silent helper.

One day he was tapping on the walls with his hammer. He started along one side and moved across the wall. After each tap he'd listen and sometimes make a mark. I didn't dare talk, straining to hear what he was listening to. I heard nothing, and when he had moved across the entire room, I finally I spoke out.

"Joseph, what are you doing?"

"I'm listening."

"Listening for what?"

Joseph put down his hammer and turned to look at me. I was afraid that this was going to be the mood my mother warned me about, but I summoned all my courage to look straight into his blue eyes. Joseph's curly brows were pushed together, and his eyes looked deeper and darker than I had ever seen. He seemed to be someplace else. I walked over and sat next to him. Joseph didn't move away, but he put down his hammer and turned his palms upward. We both just stared at the numbers on his wrists.

From somewhere deep and lonely came his voice. "I'm listening for the stories. When you have lived inside four walls for a long time, you begin to hear all its life. Some walls have too many voices. When they gave me my numbers, the walls I lived within cried at night. Sometimes I would beat on the walls trying to escape. The walls would always answer me with their pain."

I placed my small hands over Joseph's wrists and touched each number. Joseph told me that the numbers were his name while he lived inside the walls. When he finally left, he couldn't wash the numbers away, and though he tried he couldn't remove the voices from the walls.

Not too long after that day, Joseph finished putting up all the wood panels. Everywhere he had marked on the walls, he nailed the panels in. I helped with the nailing, but we never really talked after that. Our new play area was officially finished, and my parents had a party to celebrate. The basement was cozier. My mother was a great decorator, but she had failed to resolve the main problem with playing in the basement. In order to get there, you'd have to run down the stairs holding your breath so you could turn on the lights. If you think the spiders and dampness of our air raid shelter bothered me, you can bet the bogey-men I imagined hiding in the shadows made my heart race.

My sister and I would now play school in the basement. Her pretend name was Miss McGillicuddy. My fictitious name, Miss Chievous, was one that my parents always called me after I had disobeyed. One day while we were playing school, I started to hear voices. I stared at the walls, listening. My sister didn't notice, but I became agitated. Without thinking, I took a blue ink pen and began writing arithmetic problems on my left wrist. On the right wrist I wrote my name, Miss Chievous. My disobedience was too much for my sister. She ran upstairs to the safety of the living room. I forced myself to listen to the walls.

I finally came upstairs and was marched into the bathroom by my mother to wash the ink off my wrists. I didn't fight or yell. I yielded to the scrubbing, imagining myself a distinct branch of a tree growing tall, rising above to look out on the world. The stains of ink remained for another few days. Whenever my sister or my mother and I would start to fight, I'd venture down to the basement and sit quietly listening to the voices. When all signs of arguments had faded, I would brave the stairs. Joseph never came back to work at our house, but his voice was always there.

The Gilded Fish

In the 1960s during the era when racism erupted in cities, the world of the suburb dominated, and political realities shadowed the life of a goldfish.

It came as a surprise to me when I was growing up that not everyone had a Hennie in their life. Hennie was the unseen force that ruled our home. Making all wrongs right; keeping us honest. I'd come home from school and throw my books down on the counter and know by one whiff if Hennie had arrived. There would be a stillness to the rooms. As if the dust had been whisked away, leaving the walls, floors, and ceiling exposed. The crisp smell of ironing would tell me that Hennie was down in the laundry room. I'd tiptoe down, listening to her hummings of a song.

The sight of Hennie always took my breath away. She was as tall as she was broad, large and fearful until she smiled. Her mouth widened and her joy spread to her cheeks and up into her eyes. No matter how quiet I was, I never surprised Hennie. Her eyes extended back behind her kerchiefed head, knowing my every move.

"How was school today, my little girl?" she'd croon.

I'd say, "Ookaaay."

But Hennie would know that something was wrong. She could tell from the way I drew the words out that I was upset. Never once did she ask me to explain. Instead she would stand by her ironing board with her piles of white shirts and move her massive arms back and forth, humming. Her skin was smooth and slick, oiled to a chocolate sheen. I would watch, hypnotized, and slowly I'd unravel the story of my day.

Hennie was not someone you lied to. You'd have to prove you were sick if you were staying home from school. I remember wanting to skip school because of a test the next day. I moaned and groaned, trying to convince Hennie that my stomach was upset. Hennie was not being swayed by my performance, so I decided to dramatize my illness. I disappeared into the upstairs bathroom, forcing myself to regurgitate my afternoon snack. I neatly presented the evidence of my illness to her in a tall, clear glass.

Hennie's smile retreated, slipping back inside her cheeks so that her wide face became narrow and pointed, boring a hole through my lie. No words were spoken between us. I knew better than to tell my mother I was sick, because Hennie knew the truth. Instead I banished myself to my bedroom to ponder life's injustices and my own dishonesty.

Hennie was a healer, her very existence representing order and rightness. Even my mother depended on Hennie in ways that I barely understood. When Hennie was in our home, my mother was free to volunteer and go out with her girlfriends. Hennie's presence stabilized our lives.

When our goldfish became ill, it was Hennie's job to nurse it back to health. On these nights, we'd drive Hennie to the bus stop so she wouldn't have to walk carrying a fishbowl. Hennie's trip home took many hours. She'd leave our home at 5:00 p.m. and have to switch buses at least twice. I worried that the water would spill out and that the fish would die. But miraculously, Hennie would return a week later with the fish alive and well. She'd let us know when our goldfish was healthy again so we could meet her at the morning bus.

As a teenager I took the bus downtown all by myself. My mother dropped me off at the very same stop where we picked up Hennie. The bus ride through our suburb to the downtown shopping was a century long and historically revealing. The scenery changed from green and open to dark and narrow, with walls of solid buildings. The roads became cluttered and dirty. Disorder prevailed. I remember staring out the bus window wondering where in all this chaos Hennie lived.

The years passed, and one day Hennie decided she could no longer come to our home. She claimed that she was too old, and the ride on the bus was too long. Her decision coincided with the riots in the downtown neighborhoods. I no longer took the bus downtown to go shopping, fearing for my safety. I wondered if Hennie felt that same fear.

Without Hennie, our home was not the same. The sweet smells of cleanliness and hummings of truth were buried in dust balls and piles of ironing. I found my goldfish floating amidst flakes of food, bloated and unmoving. I yearned for Hennie's healing heart and tried to no avail to coax life back into my beloved fish. With tears in my eyes, I approached my mother. Expecting condolences, my heart skipped a few beats when she told me how many goldfish I had owned. My one beloved goldfish had suddenly multiplied to six. Images of Hennie painstakingly carrying our fishbowl flashed before my eyes. Solemnly I walked upstairs to the bathroom and flushed my gilded fish down the drain.

Swinging Doors

On The Art Linkletter Show, *"Kids said the darnedest things." Here is one child's memory as she works through the complexity of words and culture.*

My knees ache from kneeling on the floor, and my mouth yearns to move. But I am being ever so quiet so no one will know that I am peeping through the keyhole. I hate this door, with its solidness, its permanence. A shut door means that I am excluded. I hold my ear close to the wood, listening for words even as my eyes tear from the peering.

It was the slamming of the door that had drawn my attention. I still would be outside playing with my friends, except for the house shaking with the finality of the slam. I may be young and naïve, but once the door closed I knew that the world had narrowed. I no longer can move freely, as part of my world is cut off. I become conscious of an inside and an outside. A line has been drawn.

Sometimes I notice a door even if there isn't a physical one. The air is stale, not moving, and a hush or lull appears between words. It's as if the garage door slowly lowers and the car is caught in between. The motor is turned off, yet an incessant chatter fills the void. Without the motor running, words can't move the car forward.

I imagine all this sounds weird to you.

Imagine your best friend puts up a hand, like a stop sign. My best friend Sally sometimes does that. Even though her hand is small, I can't get by with words or even a look. I know that I will have to wait until she lowers her hand and invites me back into her thoughts. Otherwise I'd just leave. There is no use pushing on a door when it is closed.

All these thoughts swirl as I continue to peer inside the keyhole. I need to find out what is happening inside my house. I'm sneaky. Even to myself. I pretend not to care, but it bothers me that I can let Sally put up a hand, but I can't stand the slamming of a door. It is the vibration, the shaking that sends out a negative, mean signal. When it is personal and negative, I worry.

I confess that I've sometimes shut my own door, the one to the bathroom, when I want privacy. I even plug the keyhole with toilet paper so no one will see me. I'm not embarrassed, but I do feel vulnerable with my pants down. Now, if I'm in trouble, say I have the runs, I might let my mother in to help me. I trust her. I only let people I trust open the bathroom door.

Don't my parents trust me? I can't hear anything through the walls of the door. I don't think they have stuffed anything into the keyhole because I can see socks on the floor and their unmade bed. Oh—I forgot. They have two doors in their room. The second door goes into their private bathroom. I wonder why they are so closed off.

My teacher in school says she has an open door policy and that even if her door is closed, she'll let us come in. For example, if another class is inside and there is an emergency, we can come in and ask her help. If we want to talk with her after school, we can tell her anything.

I have an open door policy with Sally. I will listen to whatever she has to say, even if her hand is up. I don't put my hand up. If my hand went up, then there would be two doors shut. We might fight, but it would be worse if we didn't. I know that if I listen, sometimes her hand lowers and she smiles and all becomes well.

My knees hurt, and I feel tears staining my face. I am not crying. But it hurts that I can't see inside the second door of my parents' room. It is like I'm wearing too many layers of clothes. When I was younger my mother would make me wear an undershirt, a turtleneck polo top, a pullover sweater, one that buttoned, and then my coat to go outside to play in the snow. No one knew that I was skinny. I was someone else. I couldn't move with all the weight.

If there are too many doors to go through, too many clothes on my body, too many layers, I freeze. It is just the opposite of what my mother wanted. She thought she was making me warm and comfortable. Instead I froze in my tracks, blocked by the weight of her need.

If only I had come home earlier. Then maybe the doors wouldn't be closed. I'd be eating a peanut butter sandwich with banana slices, and my mouth would be so full that I couldn't laugh at my dad's joke. Timing is everything.

∞

Once we were going to the Department of Immigration to fill out paperwork. From what I could gather from my mother's explanation, we were from another country, even though I was born in this very house. In order for everyone to open doors of opportunity to us, we had to become citizens.

We took three buses to a tall glass building downtown. My mom told me to run, as we had to be there on time. My feet were tired from climbing all the stairs. I wasn't wearing my sneakers, or I could have gone faster. I had to be dressed up in my Sunday tight-fitting clothes with shoes that didn't bend. My mother wanted me to talk because she spoke English funny and she needed me to help out. I still can't figure out why my clothes made a difference. I don't speak with my feet.

When we got there, we waited behind a long line. I kept looking at my digital watch and the clock on the wall. I was just learning to tell time. Suddenly they pulled the glass window closed. My mom was furious. Next in line didn't count. We were shut out. I looked at my watch and banged on the window. The ladies could see me but didn't want to. My mother turned her head, but I kept knocking on the window. One of the women opened the window a crack. I said in my best English that their clock was wrong and showed her my watch.

I want to tell you that she let us finish our paperwork, but then I would be lying. Her lips were pursed, closed tight like the door. I know words came out of her mouth, but they were hollow: clogged words meant to seem nice.   I wondered if her brain was pursed as well. I could see the folds of her thoughts tied in knots. My mother smiled, as if that would open the door. I was not fooled. I understood that the folds in the woman's brain were so tight that nothing new could come in. We were wasting our time, so I took my mother's hand and coaxed her out. As we walked back to the bus stop, I looked up at the tall glass building. We could see inside, but our timing kept us out. I think it was worse than just timing. It felt like when the older kids teased me on the playground, opening the school door for me and then shutting it just as the bell rang.

Again these crazy thoughts worry me. Random feelings. My parents' shut door, Sally's raised hand, the immigration people with their rules based on a watch that misses time. I strain to see inside the keyhole. I strain to earn the right to be seen.

The house is shaking again. Or is that my knee twitching and my arms aching? I want to be inside where it is warm. I must be dreaming as the door swings open. I'm still leaning against the bottom half, but the top of the door parts and arms are reaching down to hold me. I wonder if this is real. I've only seen doors like that in books and in old movies. I wonder if this means that I am only allowed in partially.

Sally, when she is back to talking to me, when her hand is down, says that sometimes you have to protect yourself, and when you aren't sure if the person really cares, you just prop the door open. She didn't really say that, but I watch her as she makes friends with other kids and then decides not to be friends with them. When she is trying to make friends with other kids, I feel like she is not paying attention to me. It hurts my feelings because I can play with lots of people and not ignore her. I always offer her part of my lunch (the really great date-nut bread sandwich) and I smile at her a lot. Smiles are the opposite of pursing lips. A smile lifts one up and the lips part, so words and ideas can be released from the folds of the mind. Lips are connected to the heart when you smile.

My parents ignore me, but not because I did something wrong. I just don't think they know how to keep doors open. I'm serious. They didn't have to slam the door shut. I'm tired and mad now. I almost want to build a wall around myself, shut doors on them too. That won't work, because they wouldn't have the keys and they aren't as patient as I am. I am not afraid of opening doors, letting people in. I am afraid of what it means to not understand, not take the time to understand the language of a smile.

I might be imagining this, but I think I wet my pants, since I have been waiting. Something is really shaking me. I am smothering with warmth instead of cold. I hear voices. It might be nighttime, it is so dark. Maybe if I open my eyes, the door will be open and I can go back inside.

I'm not sure how this happened, but I am in my bed. I can make out faces. My mom is standing by the door to my room. My dad is standing by the window that overlooks the alley. By my side, sitting on my favorite wooden stool, is Sally. She is holding my hand. I put up my other hand and she puts up her other hand. They meet in midair. The wetness I feel are the tears that are streaming from my eyes. They are dripping on my clothes.

My mom smiles at my dad, and I hear my door close ever so softly. Everyone is inside with me. I hear three languages: Spanish, English, and the language of hands, and hugs, and smiles. My heart is open and I am full.

New Order

Putting clothes away in an overstuffed drawer, I found myself imagining the life of order and chaos. What lies behind the neat, orderly, and often pristine façade? Where within the disheveled does clarity prevail?

Arianna couldn't describe the type of furniture or the artist's paintings hanging on the walls. All she felt was the cool breeze of the room. She had no memories of this house, no point of reference, no reason to know her uncle's life. The wall to wall bookshelves were organized by topic, the novels alphabetized by author. Every book was flush except what she suspected was by design, revealing the hot topic of what was on the owner's mind. The coffee table book on Africa, with photos of the big five trophy animals, stood open. The book, *The Secret*, was turned to a special page that marked the thought, "Think the thoughts you want to be." Every financial book on making a million dollars without effort stood as a green salute to the world.

Passing her index finger along the stuffed sofa's rim, Arianna missed a dust line, the telltale sign of neglect. Unusual for a teenager to notice dirt and dust, but she wasn't the normal teen. In this room everything had its place, yet Arianna couldn't find her own. Instead of sitting on the loveseat, she lay down on the Persian rug, feeling more at home with its intricate patterns than with the stiffness of straight-back wooden chairs. She was looking for a clue of passion.

She found it tucked under the sofa, in the dark corner where cobwebs should have been: one black stocking, crumpled and forgotten. Arianna grinned with what she imagined was a huge secret. Her uncle lived alone, and unless he was living a secret life of a transvestite, it must belong to a lady friend. Could someone so neat and tidy have a lady friend? Would they kiss in a special order, first the right corner, then the left, or would they start with the widest, sweetest middle of the lips?

She felt irreverent with her sensuous thoughts in what she believed was her uncle's sanctuary. This was his library and office, not his bedroom. She stuffed the stocking in her back pocket and walked into the corridor. In her house she had hallways, small walkways to rooms only ten feet away. Here the corridors were lined with dark mahogany wood and stretched for a long echo. Arianna felt her existence with the clunk of her heel. Presence: everything designed to reverberate back to oneself.

She tiptoed down to the room assigned to her by the housekeeper. Since her mother's passing and her father's disappearance, any space with walls was better than the hole she had placed herself in. The door took only a nudge to open. The smell of lemons greeted her. At first she thought the smell was from an air-freshener or cleanser, but the smell came from a tall glass of lemonade placed by the window. Even the bedspread with its lemon tree design had been washed in lemon juice.

Arianna allowed herself one teardrop before she downed the lemonade, placed the glass on the window sill, and pulled the covers off the bed. She needed to surround herself in a mess to match her chaotic emotions.

Anger, fear, loss wound into a tight ball behind her belly button. The cord of connection to the world, an elastic band pulled taut. Arianna couldn't say why, but the tragic turn in her life didn't come as a surprise.

This house did, and trying to understand how her uncle could actually be her mother's brother threw Arianna into a proper tizzy.

She unzipped her suitcase. Smashed together, stuffed inside, were the remnants of fifteen years of carefree living, fifteen years that she took for granted. She and her mother had been only twenty years apart in their life cycles, but her mother died at thirty-five, way before a midlife crisis. Arianna didn't have a name for the crisis she was now experiencing. She fumbled through the clothes and pulled out the framed photograph of her mother and father, smiling back at her. She loved her dad's crooked lips. The left side always tilted a little farther up when he was happy, as if the right side had a hard time keeping up with his joy. Her mother's eyebrows smiled more than her lips. Whenever she danced, sang, or wrote in deep concentration, the right brow slipped upward in anticipation of life. These were her parents' "tells." In this picture the two of them were digging out a culvert filled with debris, with their farm as a backdrop; their smudged faces and filthy clothes told her all was right in the world.

But it wasn't. Arianna was six when that picture was taken, and the next year she was the one outside digging debris with her mother. Her father had vanished from their lives. No explanations, no crying, but Arianna noticed that her mom's eyebrows moved closer together as if life had them perpetually locked in a worried embrace. The farm took all their time, yet her mom still danced, sang, and wrote. She hugged Arianna lots and told her how much she reminded her of her dad.

Arianna dumped the rest of the suitcase contents on her uncle's guest bed. She carried her toothbrush, shampoo, and conditioner into the bathroom. She needn't have bothered, as the bathroom was fit for a queen. Her uncle had thought of needs she didn't know she had. Arianna pulled open the top drawer to find shiny foil, a bottle of dark liquid that reeked of sulfur. On the label a smiling woman with long, flowing blond hair enticed Arianna with her eyes, luring Arianna to change her own look to hers. She needn't have bothered, since Arianna had chopped off her dark brown locks the year her dad disappeared. Arianna had no choice, as the tangled mess was his job. Before bedtime he'd comb out the twigs, insects, and flowers, commenting on her day's adventures. Afterwards her mom was too preoccupied, too sad, to take over his ritual. By choice Arianna left it short with just wisps of curls

Behind the hair dye, a hair brush with an ivory handle and bristles that tickled her face lay next to a matching hand mirror with the initials A.R. engraved on the handle. Her heart skipped a beat when she realized that these were her initials if you called her by her given name, not her nickname Airy. Somewhere along the way her mother had shortened Arianna Reece Wilcox to Airy. She said it fit her personality.

She didn't feel airy now. Her heart sank inside her chest. Arianna knew this room was meant to make her feel comfortable, but instead she felt as if she would spoil some effect, the idea of grace. Arianna continued on her quest of discovery. The bottom drawer was stuck. She had to push her right foot against the floor board to get enough leverage to pull it open. It held bobby-pins, curlers, and a hair dryer with a plastic cover attached to a hose. She put the plastic cap on her head and suddenly she got it. All of these things had been her mom's. The initials on the ivory mirror were hers, Annabelle Reece. This had been her room when she was growing up. The family estate she never talked about was now her home.

Staring in the mirror, Arianna saw what her uncle would eventually see when she finally met him: the raccoon eyes of a farm girl with the awkward body of a sapling tree that was too thin to withstand wind and rain. Did he know how stubborn her roots were, that she dug her heels down deep and that she couldn't possibly fit into his orderly life?

Arianna pulled the black stocking she had discovered in his study from her back pocket, let the silky fibers roll through her thumb and pointer finger. Guiltily she pulled it over her hand and slid it onto her right foot and up her calf. Her mother once wore stockings. Ariana never had. Were stockings, elegant dresses expected of her? Her best jeans, frayed at the knee and worn thin in the butt, were her old uniform.

The knock on the door was so faint that Arianna mistook it for an insistent woodpecker. She pulled the stocking off her foot, rolled down her pant leg, and went to open the door. She wasn't quite ready to meet anyone. She wasn't ready to fold into the neat creases of this life. When she pulled the door open, the housekeeper stood with her knuckles poised to tap with more force. She could tell from the pursed lips that both her tardiness and abruptness displeased the woman.

"I've come to fetch you, as Mr. Reese would like you to join him in the garden."

Adrianna half curtsied, not knowing what else to do. And then to make matters worse, she hit her forehead with the palm of her hand. The housekeeper raised her eyebrow and then hid her hand over her mouth, covering what Adrianna imagined was her version of a fit of the giggles.

"You must think I'm a complete idiot. Please tell me your name so I don't feel like I'm living in the middle of someone else's life. To tell you the truth, I think I'm living a nightmare."

"I'm Ms. Stone, and I've worked for Mr. Reese for twelve years. He is a nice man. I'm sorry for your loss. If this is a nightmare to you, then I hope you wake up soon to find it a pleasant dream."

Her words were meant to comfort Arianna, yet they stung. Arianna couldn't tell if the housekeeper was a wasp or a honey bee. She never minded getting stung by a honey bee, as she knew they were protecting the sweet nectar of the honeycomb. Wasps, on the other hand, were more concerned with their own survival. Perhaps it was she who was the wasp.

"Can I find him on my own? I'm not quite ready to meet him."

"Suit yourself. He is in the third garden to the left."

Arianna closed the door and rested her back against it. Three gardens, well, that said it all. Her parents had one farm and no garden. Everything they planted, they ate. The luxury of adornment was trumped by nature's demands. Their days were regulated, not only by the rising sun, but by the harvest moon, the monsoon rains, and the golf balls of hail. She let out the royal Reese sigh. One like her mother's exasperated slow exhalation that punctuated the air when they had tied up the bean vines and the wind knocked them down again. If she was to meet her uncle, Arianna had no choice about seeing the gardens.

She abandoned her efforts in the bathroom and returned to her suitcase. Hanging up her wilted and wrinkled clothing wouldn't make her look any better, but at least Adrianna could survey the situation and perhaps create a sense of style. The doors to the closet opened outward into the bedroom. Her fingers still held onto the knob when she felt the sun kiss her. The closet walls were of varying shades of yellow, pale and dusty like the sprinkles of bee pollen, then vibrant and almost blinding like the pot of gold at the end of the rainbow. A small skylight filtered in the real rays of hope, but nothing was left to chance. The smell of citrus again, as if a lemon tree had been planted in every corner of the room, even here in this hidden space. Sunshine and lemons, those too were her mother's essence.

Outside the bedroom window, the monotonous din of a motor, too soft for a tractor. Theirs had broken down the week before her mother died. It might have been what killed her. She had insisted on fixing everything herself, even though she wasn't feeling well. Her simple cold was really masking pneumonia, which Arianna was to find out later was masking lung cancer. Arianna handed her the tools, even took the motor apart, but her mother still knew more than her. Arianna bowed to her stubborn temper, her insistence on finishing the job. Without the tractor, they couldn't farm. Without her mother, she couldn't breathe.

Arianna knew she had been procrastinating when the hum of the lawn motor stopped. Looking out at the now-manicured lawn, she stripped off her tattered and love-worn jeans, rushed into the shower and lathered herself in lemon-scented shampoo and body wash. With towels so soft that she barely felt their touch, she returned to the closet. The sun rays flashed off something hanging in the corner of the closet, the perfect outfit. She pulled the blue-jean overalls off the hanger and held them in front of her body. These, too, must have been my mother's, the sister of her uncle, the woman she never suspected of keeping secrets. With thousands of precise stitches her mother had altered the pockets to create a living garden. One pocket held the sun, one rows of lemon trees, another was covered with bees swarming flowers, and the last pocket remained bare.

Arianna slipped the overalls over her hips and clasped the buckle at the top. She smiled at her image. Somewhere in her bundle of clothes she found a banana-colored t-shirt and a wild green-leafed bandanna. She could almost hear her mother's laughter at the sight of her, feel her father tousling the brown curls peeking out from the bandanna. Arianna was ready to meet her uncle. She took one long deep breath and whispered, "Ready or not, here I come."

The air was warm, warmer than she expected. Their farm was hot enough to grow oranges, bananas, lemons, avocadoes, tomatoes, and at least two crops of all the other vegetables. Here the temperature was moderate, she guessed close to 70 degrees. Only 200 miles separated them, yet Florida was a surprising state, tropical but with a twist. Arianna could tell just by looking at the trees that they were in a different growing belt. Absent were the feather-like palm trees.

The first garden area controlled her, leading her to a red brick pathway through a stone archway that flowed into a series of overlapping red oak trees. Arianna felt as if she were back in her uncle's study, uncomfortable with the coiffed hedges pruned so that every leaf obeyed. Here there were no surprises, the trees aligned equidistant and the flowering rose bushes interspersed at the exact spot, each bloom the proper red. Yet she had to admit that the order left no questions. Here, her emotions would always be steady, calm, the same. Walking through this garden Arianna would never get lost. As if on cue, a white iron-rimmed table and chairs appeared, set with a pitcher of lemon water and clear plastic notebook and pen, the perfect spot to sit and write.

Beyond the table, the path began to change. The red bricks morphed into large stone slabs, fitted together with sedges for the seams. She sensed that the next garden would be beyond the cascading stone ledges that served for steps leading downward toward a gateway. The gate was left ajar, inviting Arianna to step inside. She did. To her amazement, her eyes saw only the stems of trees. The contorted stems of the hazelnut felt like her insides. She paused to look at the bright red tips of new growth on the dogwood trees, their flowers reaching upward to the heavens. And then there was yellow, the golden willow with its glowing amber bark.

Even though Arianna knew that the second garden was carefully planned by her uncle, there was a sense of happenstance, where the haphazard nature of plants dominated. She felt a softening of the gnarly tightness behind her belly button. Her heart beat stronger.

Gradually the stones changed to small pebbles, the paths narrowing until she came to a low white picket fence. Painted across the gate were words she had heard before: *The order of the world is chaos.* Her mother and father had always told Arianna that she was their chaos.

There he was, her uncle, bent down by the hopeful snowdrops, the pussy willows that popped out beyond his head. She would have recognized him in a minute. His back hunched just like her mom's. Kneeling, he revealed the bottom of his boots, immaculate except for stray clippings from the path, wild weeds entwined inside the tire tracks of his soles.

His gardening uniform included a floppy mustard hat that covered the back of his neck. Her mom had almost an identical one, but hers was the color of robin eggs. His pants wicked water and repelled mud, and even with the heat he appeared cool. Arianna watched as sprinklers sprayed mist over him, and he cajoled chickweed free from the earth. To him, the water and dirt were nonexistent, rolling off so he remained Mr. Clean.

She didn't know how to make her feet go forward. They were stuck on the wrong side of the fence. Beads of sweat stung her eyes. She wasn't crying. Arianna refused to cry as panic choked her voice, froze her hands, and held her tight. The wind must have had sympathy for her, as its rustling made her uncle turn toward her.

"Well, there you are, Airy. I was hoping you'd pay me a visit. Come on, I won't bite, open the gate and come on through."

He gently unfolded his body and stood up. Arianna watched as he meticulously brushed himself off, making sure that the garden remained on the earth. He was tall, taller than her mom by at least half a foot, towering over her. Arianna stared down at his feet and finally looked up to see his face. And there it was, the eyebrows pulled together, then softened, then pulled together, waiting for her. She could see her mother's arms holding her tight, feel her embrace. She hoped that there was space between the furrows for her.

The fence gate creaked, which made Arianna smile at the flaw. She made a mental note not to oil it. She hoped her uncle agreed. Before she had taken more than five steps, his long legs came to meet her.

"I don't suppose you remember me. I used to pick you up and twirl you in the air. Your mom always told me to stop, that I'd make you dizzy like I used to do to her when we were kids. You are too big now for me to do that."

She longed for the twirl, although her memory was that of her father twirling her, never her uncle.

"You look like my mom, sort of. I didn't think you would."

"Perhaps you thought I would look like a monster, or perhaps a model of perfection. That would be worse, wouldn't it? Your mom used to scold me so for my neatness."

He took the thoughts straight from her head, and she was rendered speechless. It was her turn now to talk. What could she possibly do or say that would take this awkwardness away?

"I don't really remember you. My mom hardly talked about her family. I thought she had a falling out or something."

He stood there with a half-smile on his face, reminding her of her dad's. The one her father used to conceal something from her mom, the one that sometimes wasn't really a smile, but a long story. Stories told behind closed doors, often with yelling, and then silence.

This silence with her uncle stretched so long that Arianna could hear the bees buzzing and the fluttering wings of butterflies as they circled the flowers. She wanted to disappear, but instead she walked deeper down the pathway until she came to the smell of yellow. Her uncle followed. A sweet, light citrus fragrance led her to a small greenhouse. Inside, three miniature lemon trees stood as if to salute her. Each had a name, Annabelle, Arianna, and Andrew.

"I see you found them."

"Uncle Andrew, what did I find? I can call you

Uncle Andrew, can't I?"

"You found your mother's experiment. And, yes, you can call me Uncle Andrew, although you once called me Uncle Amazing."

Something clicked inside, a flashback to a visitor at their house. Her dad hadn't disappeared yet from their life, and her uncle was always at the farm. He'd be outside in the fields with her mom, talking. She could almost hear her mom's voice, "That is amazing—do you think we could actually grow that in miniature?" Or, "Amazing how when we keep the roots balled, the lemons produce quicker." Whenever her uncle was at the house, everything was amazing.

All she could think to say was, "Where did Uncle Amazing go?"

"Come with me. The greenhouse is too hot for me to answer. Let's walk some more in your mom's garden. Did you know that she started it when she was your age?"

Arianna tried to picture her mom at fifteen living in her pristine room, walking down the smooth hallways and outside to this greenhouse. She had worked on the farm under her mom's direction, never once thinking to experiment in the science of growing. The mother she knew hummed to herself, passed hours in the fields, and read late into the night. She'd make her a rolled-out crust for a special treat. Flour often left its imprint on her nose and her clothes. She'd present a heart-shaped baked crust with cinnamon and sugar sprinkles as if it were the most elegant dessert. And it was. They'd devour every last crumb.

"What ever possessed her to grow miniature lemon trees?"

"I'm guilty of that. You see, my father in his infinite wisdom sent me to horticulture school. I had other ideas of how my life would go, but I hated to disappoint him. Your mother was my sidekick. If she could have gone to school, well, we might have already put miniature fruit trees on the market. I was a reluctant rebel with opportunity. She was just a rebel."

"You mean she gave all this up because she met my dad."

"How did you come up with that? You've got it backwards. Your dad encouraged her to stay, even if our father wouldn't pay for her formal education. It was I who wanted to leave. I wanted to pursue music. Your mom felt so guilty."

"But what made her leave?"

"She thought she was protecting me, by trying to force my father to let me go to music school. She only made matters worse. Neither of us got what we wanted. I caved in, and your mom felt like an outcast."

Arianna walked towards a section of the garden filled with honeybees. They swarmed around a bush of pink flowers. She closed her eyes and heard her mom humming. There were no words to her hum, but a melodious buzzing merged to form a garden song. Always, when she worked out in the garden, she would create the music of the day. Now Arianna realized that this was her uncle's song.

"You are a song writer, aren't you?"

Arianna didn't expect to hear laughter. Her uncle was bent over laughing, as if she had said the funniest thing. His eyes glistened, his lips parted in animation, and she remembered the sock.

Despite his laughter, his voice came out hard, edged in cynicism. "No, I'm a landscaper and an entrepreneur."

She expected more of an answer. His short response negated the laughter, made her feel as if he was sinister. His abruptness snapped her to attention, and she felt awkward all over again. She realized how much he had hated compromising, giving in to his father. His resentment was clear.

"Landscapers create order. The entrepreneur's only thought is to create more money." His words were said with a punctuation that didn't allow for questions.

"You can't mean that. I don't believe you. Looking out from my room, my mother's old room upstairs, it all looks perfect, ordered, controlled. From above it looks scary to me, sterile. But now that I've walked through these gardens, seen you amongst them, I hear songs. Only a musician would even hear the rhythms in the patter of rain on a rock, or the harmony of the birds and the bees. You would never sell this garden. Maybe you can sell the sterile stuff, but not to true gardeners. I think you design things with music in mind."

"Ah yes, you have my sister's insight, but no history. Your mother was almost the only one who could see through me."

"And the other person, Uncle Andrew?"

"She is long gone."

His eyebrows rose up and curled into one another. No space, only the tightness of memory. Adrianna fumbled for the black stocking stashed in her back pocket, feeling the lub-dub of old lovers' hearts beating. Her own was thumping behind the bibbed coveralls of another time. She steeled herself for an angry outburst, but couldn't help herself. Her uncle, still a stranger, had her mom inside. She wasn't afraid of family.

"I think I found something of that other person."

Arianna held the black stocking out to her Uncle. He didn't meet her hands, only stared with an open mouth. She could hear the breath expelled, the inhale of emotions. Not a sound from the birds, bees, or the wind. The silence that bound him was both hot and cold. Perspiration filled the creases on his forehead. Her hands froze in place, shook out his memories.

She had lost her chance, lost her nerve as she watched her uncle turn his back to her, walk away from her mother's garden. Each step took him up the path, up closer to his controlled spaces where the lines of his life would be back in order. Arianna couldn't allow that. She ran after him, jumping over bushes, and rocks.

"Uncle Amazing, wait up. You can't disappear, you can't stop talking just because you're upset. You can't make me any sadder than I already am."

"That is enough. You're dismissed."

∞

Arianna ran past her uncle with the speed of a tornado. She trampled on some of the plants, bumped into the bushes. Her ears rang with echoes of the dismissal. Never had she ever argued with her mother. Never had she felt so abandoned. The death of her mother at least carried memories, but her uncle's dismissal slammed her heart.

With muddy feet, she stomped up the stairs to her room. She threw her shoes against the wall, ripped off the overalls, and slipped under the covers. She craved sleep.

Hours later she woke to an insistent knock. She rolled over in bed, pulled the pillows on top of her head. The lemon smell seemed fainter. The aroma of food filled the room. She lifted herself up to find Ms. Stone with a tray of food.

"Time to eat something. You've slept through dinner, and I suspect if I didn't come up, you'd sleep through breakfast too."

Confused, Arianna looked at the window. The drapes were drawn.

"What time is it?"

"Time for you to stop brooding and eat."

"Did my uncle ask for me?"

"Should he?"

Arianna thought again about the wasp and the bee.

"I made him angry. He dismissed me. I don't think I should be here."

"Mr. Reese is a complicated man. He mourns so many losses. And to answer your first question, he didn't ask for you."

Again the stinging words, but Arianna looked at Ms. Stone straight on. She had a smile wider than a watermelon, red gums bright against her white teeth. Arianna accepted the tray of biscuits and eggs.

"If you have time, will you sit with me while I eat?"

"Just for a minute. I have a household to run, and worrying about a teenager isn't usually on my list. Mr. Reese left early this morning, as he does every morning. I expect he'll return in a foul mood and hungry."

"Oh, where does he go?"

"He visits someone."

"Why does he visit the same person every day and come back angry? My mom said that to repeat a bad experience is to punish yourself. "

"Well, Ms. Arianna, you mom was a wise woman. She and your uncle were very close. Each deals with loss differently."

Arianna finished the breakfast biscuits and handed Ms. Stone the tray. "Thanks, that was good. I liked the marmalade. It tastes like something my mom would make."

"Lunch is the main meal in this house. I start cooking in about an hour. You can help if you'd like, unless you want to stay in bed."

Arianna nodded at the challenge. After Ms. Stone left, she slipped out of bed and opened the drapes to the morning sun. Despite the bright rays, she still felt the gloom of yesterday. She found sunglasses in one of the drawers, wound a scarf around her tossed curls, and threw her mother's overalls on.

Knowing her uncle was off and with only one hour to explore, Arianna walked along the corridors, looking for clues. Something connected her to her uncle besides her mother. She remembered Ms. Stone saying that everyone deals with losses differently. What losses beside her mother did her uncle have?

Her mother had often said that walls talk. At Arianna's house the walls had been filled with pictures of her growing up. There used to be ones of her father and mother and the family, but when her father disappeared, they came down. Her mother painted over the faded areas and said they needed a new story. In the corridors of her uncle's house, each wall held paintings of landscapes, gardens, or newspaper articles. Most of the articles were about World War II or the Vietnam War, talking about the beginning or end of troubled times.

Arianna roamed into the den next to the living room where she had found the stocking. As neat and orderly as the living room had been, this room felt like a trash can turned upside down and rifled through. This was where she found the pain. Frame marks stained the walls, fragments of newspaper articles were crumpled in the garbage can, and a desk strewn with pictures told her of her uncle's loss.

She found a picture of five people—her parents,

herself, her uncle, and a beautiful woman with blond hair. Arianna was a toddler held in her mother's arms, her father stood next to the woman on one side, and her uncle on the other. A series of pictures, mostly of her uncle and the woman, but some were torn up. In these, only her father's photo had been ripped free.

Arianna closed the door to the room. She couldn't breathe. Her breakfast came rising up, and she ran outside to regurgitate her fears. Confused tears fell silently as she searched for some memory of her father. Her mother never said anything about her father after he disappeared. She worked so hard to keep Arianna insulated and free.

She slipped into the kitchen exactly one hour from her waking. Ms. Stone nodded. "Start chopping the apples. We'll need them for the pie. When you get done with that, I could use some help with the vegetables for the soup. I'm working on the lamb shank. It will be a feast, even if your uncle comes in late."

When Arianna answered with only a nod, Ms. Stone looked at her sternly. "You have the look of a ghost who saw another ghost. Be careful, young lady, you could really make yourself sad. I suggest you be yourself and stop prying into sadness."

"Will you answer my questions?"

"Remember, I'm here as a cook and helper, not seer. I take care of the physical needs, and the other isn't up to me."

"Am I supposed to be here with my uncle? Would my mom want that for me?"

"I'm no mind reader, but your mother and brother were best of friends, even after the accident. So, yes, you are supposed to be here."

Arianna chopped the apples and the vegetables,

cleaned her mess, and took the remnants into the compost. She sat in the tidiest of the gardens and thought about an accident she knew nothing of. She chose not to ask about it.

Lunch came and went without the appearance of her uncle. Arianna stayed clear of the house and roamed along the edges of the garden, not wanting to venture anywhere near yesterday's dismissal.

But when dinner came and went without her uncle, she felt drawn to her mother's lemon tree garden. She ran down the paths and found her uncle by the second gate, near the table with the neatly laid pitcher of water and writing paper. He was sitting down staring at her as she came huffing up.

"Arianna, I'm sorry. Yesterday, you caught me off guard."

She didn't want to talk to him, didn't want to worry about saying the right thing, or making him comfortable. He was always making himself comfortable. Arianna did the only thing she knew worked for her. Humming her mother's garden song, she placed the silk black stocking in his hand, took off his floppy yellow hat, and kissed the top of his head.

"You've got the tune all wrong. When I wrote it for your mother, there were more dark notes, more thunder and lightning. Your version is lighter."

"Did you write it when my dad left us?"

"Yes and no. Your dad never left you. Well, not on purpose. I wrote the song after the accident. Your father was driving my fiancée back here when a car hit them. Your dad's body was never found. We assume he drowned in the river and died instantly. My fiancée, well, she suffered awhile, and then slipped into a coma. I haven't written any music since then."

His words sank into the air. The leaves rustled,

whispering, "Accident. He died." A woodpecker tapped sharply, "Died, died, dead."

The knots Arianna had felt earlier returned. But they had moved from behind her belly button, up into her chest. The tightness squeezed out a gasp, and the welled-up tears mixed to create the sounds of a thunderstorm. Her fists pounded against her uncle's back.

Between her sobs, Arianna heard herself scream, "How could you disappear like that? Left my mom and me to suffer! Why didn't you come to the farm?"

He let her pummel her anger until her fury dissipated. He turned and caught her hands, locked his gaze into hers. "I couldn't face your mother afterwards. I suspected the worst of your father and my fiancée. Their absences didn't make sense once we heard the news of the accident. Too much was at stake, too many questions. There was no one to explain what happened. Neither your mom nor I knew what to think. My fiancée is still in a coma."

The meekest of "Oh's" came from her lips. Arianna didn't know what to say. She sank down into one of the chairs by the table, fingered the pen and writing paper. She had been wrong telling her uncle that she couldn't be sadder.

He reached across the table for her hand and squeezed it ever so gently. She closed her eyes and felt her mother's soft hands reaching for her, the firm hand of her father helping her up from a fall. Arianna squeezed back and opened her eyes to her uncle's tentative, crooked smile, his eyebrows wide open waiting for her.

"My mom told me he disappeared. There wasn't a burial for my father."

"He did disappear. I guess that is why I did, too."

A tree frog nestled in the shadow of a tree began its song. The chirp of crickets followed. The woodpecker tapped in sets of rapid threes. The scent of lemons came from a light breeze, leaving the wisp of citrus.

Arianna stood up. She wanted to go back to her mom's old bedroom, sit with the yellow, the light, the smells of lemon and the past. She wanted to make her bed, take a nap, and then find needle and thread. The last pocket on her mom's coveralls would have musical notes.

"Airy."

"Yes, Uncle Amazing."

"Your mom and dad were right. You are Chaos. They have given me the best gift."

From Here to There

Moved by a postcard, a snapshot of another way of life, I entered inside the picture to an imagined world.

I am lost amongst the images hidden behind colors, somewhere in the time of life. From here to there and everywhere, my story starts with brilliant color, a series of dyes made from the plant extracts of the jungle: yellows, greens, reds, hues of sand dust, pollen, grassy reeds, and faded bark.

When I was small, my grandma would part my jet-black hair down the center of my head, a division so precise that my vision became sharp, eyes focused on the minutiae of the world revealed. Twisting the silky strains between worn hands, she braided my hair to create a royal crown upon my head. I became the queen of our fruited patch of land.

Our house was a modest one-room affair. White stucco washed daily until I took red dye and painted the courtyard a vibrant red. As queen over sovereign land, I was powerful yet kind. Each morning before my chores, I sat in my court overseeing my loyal subjects, banana trees and green-feathered palm trees. I commanded the breeze to whip through their fronds, cooling the courtyard, making shadow playmates who obeyed my every wish. The unconscious dedication was rewarded with gifts of sweet yellow slices of heaven.

Even as a queen, I obeyed a higher force. My grandmother had strict rules to follow. Tend to the plants and then hurry to do the wash. I was too small to carry the clothes atop my head, so I followed behind. More times than not I'd take a shortcut to the riverbanks through the aqueduct. My grandmother called the tunnel "man's folly." But I had faith that one day water would flow and that the world would change. Until then I watched the sun follow me inside as my image grew to gigantic proportions. I ran, seeing myself larger than life. I saw my future just steps ahead.

Massive rocks, boulders worn by wind and the power of turbulent waters, shouldered the riverbanks. Cut into the rock was the river's story. I knew where the river had been, but always wondered where it was going.

A yellow skiff waited patiently for me. But I denied its call, until that one morning. Instead of watching the fisherman come and go, I crawled inside and hid behind the fishing nets. I held my breath as the nets were taken out one by one. With each heave I was more exposed. I closed my eyes and prayed to the god of sun and water that I would be invisible. Luck was with me. When I opened my eyes, before me stood my grandfather. He was the skiff's owner. From that day on I traveled down the river, abandoning my queenly chores. I learned the songs of the river: the silence in the dry season, the roar after the rains. I could hear the sun bake the skin of the rocks, the sigh as vapor escaped into the air. I saw rainbows in water drops. I had no need of the sky until the black of night set in. Then the stars befriended me.

It was the absence of color that forced my eyes to see inside the stars. Nightly I allowed the reds and greens and blues to mingle. I could hear their calls. The red popping of fire, the swish of green reeds, the whisper of blue wind along my face. My story continues forever, meandering with the river, the black night, the daily rituals. Somewhere amongst the colors I aged, but I assure you that you can find me from here to there.

Sleep-Over

A child's memory of a grandmother's house unravels a woman's history. Present and future sleep-overs promise new revelations and hopes.

I remember the porch swing in the front of Bubbie's house where we would sit, rocking back and forth, while she picked the stems off the green beans. Paisley runners lined the inside foyer. Steep stairs circled around the bottom floor up to the bedroom and the cordoned-off area for the renter.

I didn't dare mount for fear of what might be hiding beyond the cord past our bedrooms. Holding my small suitcase, I counted twenty-eight steps until I reached the room I shared with my Bubbie. Two twin beds with identical blue blankets, folded under crisply starched white sheets. This became my dream spot. Between the snores of my Bubbie and the distant chug-a-lug and toots of the train, I dreamed of unknown adventures.

The kitchen is where life happened. Every meal had its ritual. The day began with hot lemon-water to wash the system clean, sipped from a saucer to cool, a sugar cube between the teeth to mix sour with sweet. Rice Krispies snapped, crackled, and popped with cream and bananas. Exactly at noon we'd share a hot bowl of chicken soup with *farvela,* tiny pocket noodles. Often we passed the morning making *matzo balls*, the Jewish version of dumplings. For me this was heaven. Everything we did had a purpose, and the very act of eating meant you had worked and learned. We travelled to the fish-market where Bubbie held and smelled the fish. She had some magical way of knowing what would be best for boiling her famous *gefilte fish*. Even the tablecloth that graced the metal kitchen table told me stories. None of the stains earned a reprimand from an adult, but rather were a symbol of the day's activity. Bubbie folded the tablecloth for a clean spot until white no longer existed. She knew all that she had cooked and eaten for the week, and celebrated finally by bringing out a clean cloth for the Sabbath. I learned that messes were made to clean up and that conservation meant nothing was wasted. I felt more at home here on my sleepovers than I did at home with my parents' contemporary way of life.

With Bubbie as my role model, I entered the sixties understanding social injustices, the big ideas of immigration for reasons of persecution, and the horrible consequences of racial profiling. Two conversations stay with me. One concerned my grandfather Abraham, who died before I was born but left me the honor of his name.

"Bubbie, tell me about Grandpa Abe. No one speaks of him, and I need to know."

Her look went distant, as if she had traveled back to a time where life hurt, where the choices didn't exist. "We both emigrated from Kiev. Your Uncle Joe sponsored Abraham. Joe dated my sister, Lena. A nice man, short, a mechanic, I learned to love him." Simple facts, simple ways explained the complex world of hate, the demands of society. Bubbie's answer gave me her decision. She chose learning to love.

The second conversation still haunts me. During the time of racial strife in Baltimore, Bubbie took a bus from the suburbs to an adjacent city, Pimlico. While she shopped, some hooligans mugged her, stealing her purse and leaving her lying on the pavement. During her recovery, Bubbie stayed with my family in our new home.   As I massaged her sore muscles and aching hands, she told me this story. "I didn't know the black boys who hit me. They are bad."

I swallowed hard, remembering when the two of us used to collect her rental fees in the seedier side of town. We would bring home-baked cookies to her tenants. "Bubbie, you don't mean blacks are bad, do you? You can't mean your renters are bad, they love you."

Her eyes welled up, and a shadow crossed over her. I held my breath, not wanting her to declare a whole population bad. I needed her to love the world in which we live. I needed her to make a choice.

"All I know is that my tenants are all black and all nice. These boys were black and bad. Fear is ugly. It has no color."

∞

At age sixteen my family moved to Miami, Florida. If I thought my life odd in the suburbs of Baltimore, living in Miami was a jump into glitz and glamour. To keep sane, I chose to pass summers with my Bubbie. I thought then and until recently that I was born in the wrong generation, that my Mom was a socialite, a caring woman who preferred the finer things, and that there must have been a mistake at the hospital—a warp in time—or maybe I had been switched at birth with a farmer's child.

I was wrong. I look like both of my parents, and I have the short stature of my Bubbie and Grandpa Abe. My Bubbie passed away at age 82. I raced to the hospital in Baltimore from my home in Puerto Rico, to just miss saying good-bye. Our sleepovers had ended with a finality that only healed with my dreams of Bubbie looking out and over me.

∞

Bubbie still proves to me that I am of her and of my mother. That by being wrong, I learn. This summer my mother—now eight-five, or if we use her system of counting, fifteen years beyond whatever years I claim for my age—slept at my home. A five-week sleep-over, on our twenty acres, isolated from her bridge games, stores, and friends. She thrived. Yes, she still smoked her cigarettes, dressed in designer everything, wore makeup, sparkled with diamonds, and loved her glass of Chardonnay. Beyond those tendencies, I found a woman who pays attention.

Now living in Palm Springs along a golf course, she has a gardener who takes care of her grounds and Stella who cleans her house. Yet she marvels at the ginger bloom in our greenhouse, with its white waxy comb, and then the small, delicate yellow flowers that nub their way out. Her smoking sanctuary, created by my husband, includes a glass ashtray and an overhang in case of rain. It faces our raised beds of lettuce, carrots, beets, leeks, shallots, and ever-growing delphiniums. My mom worries when a baby robin falls from its nest and the mother robin no longer feeds it worms. Not used to the absence of television, she downloads book after book from Amazon. She engages in political conversations with my husband.

I see my Bubbie in her depth. More sophisticated, yet simple in acceptance. We talk of Bubbie's grocery stores, my own store, and my mom's real estate deals. She shies away from questions about my grandfather's past. She confesses that as a teenager, she was more concerned with getting out of the house than wondering about the history of her father's life before arriving in the United States. One memory finally ekes out, "I remember seeing my father in our library crying. He was reading a letter saying his cousin had just died. He was the last of his family members still alive. All others had been wiped out by religious cleansing."

I see bridges between the generations, the independent streak, and the stubborn and intense sense of survival in the world that presents hurdles. My Bubbie, brilliant but illiterate in English, never could read, no matter how many times I helped her, finger pointing at letters, sounding out words from my Nancy Drew books. But my mother sits on our brown overstuffed chair with a blanket warming her cold feet, reading her Kindle tablet, ten hours a day. As a child I buried my head in a book, my way of escaping and learning. Now I write stories. My mom reads my work with her critical eye and, with a twinkle in her eye, encourages me to include more sex scenes.

And to my delight, our kitchen unites us with rituals. Jim makes sauces from our tomatoes, basil, oregano, onions. He rolls out homemade noodles. Every meal is planned. My mom chooses to snip the tops off the green beans after each of our garden harvests. Instead of rocking on the porch, she takes a seat at the kitchen counter. As she puts it, "This is better than the food channel, for entertainment." I bake the recipe my Bubbie shared with me when I was only ten, *Mandel brot,* the Jewish version of biscotti.

After meals my mom and I wash the dishes. I purposefully leave her to the drying and putting away. After five weeks she knows where the cheese grater rests, where the salad dressing mixer belongs. Jim watches us from the dining room as we take a break and dance the cha-cha-cha. He stifles a laugh at our rendition of the salsa and the twist.

When my kids arrive, they embrace their grandmother, identifying with her smart clothes and finesse. I'm their hippie mother, a little too earthy for their present tastes. They circle my mother and ply her with questions. Not of her past, but seeking a window of understanding of how I was raised. They leave on shopping adventures or on a quick trip to the casino. They see in their grandmother an accomplished woman who knows nuances of real estate and the financial elements of business. They click.

∞

Five weeks flew by. The longest sleep-over I've had with anyone. The longest my mother has stayed with me since I left home forty-two years ago. I needed the five weeks to see Bubbie in my mother. Underneath all of her daily rituals, my mom sees with her heart, ponders life without distractions. She didn't just visit me; she slipped over into my world.

Now that she is gone back to her home in the desert, our home feels emptier. Someday my children will have kids of their own. I await the arrival of grandkids, the advent of many sleep-overs. I never did find out about the renter in my Bubbie's house, a mystery my mother claimed not to remember. I can feel the small, soft hands of future grandkids entwined in mine as we walk in our woods. I can almost hear their squeals at the howl of a coyote, the hoots of an owl. They'll dream their own adventures, as the train chug-a-lugs at half-past eleven each night.

Maturing

Five Kids and a Dog

Children play without judging the world they are in. They adapt situations to their reality and transform simple events into profound insights.

Woody, David, Lionel, Otis, and Oscar run to the sound of my voice: "Maya, Maya, come. Good girl, come."

I've trekked a mile down from the gravel driveway of my home and into the high weeds of the adjacent property. As the crow flies, the house abuts our six acres, but with a ravine and deep woods between, I rarely visit. With a green leash in hand, I've been calling after my seven-year-old black lab who has once again escaped from the house to be the hunter of her dreams.

Woody, who is really Willy, comes running over to me. His t-shirt is ripped across the chest, exposing the round belly of a toddler. David, his brother who is twice his size (two times my knee height), catches up and holds Willy's hand.

"That your dog?"

"Yeah, is she bothering you?"

"Nah, we guys have been playing with her all day."

"Can you help me catch her?"

"Nah, she chases everything she sees. Look, she's off again."

I hurry my pace and leap through the weeds, past the chicken coop and wired fence, and find myself facing a thicket. I'm not about to go foraging the woods for Maya. I turn back to find ten eyes staring at me.

"What's she chasing?"

I bow my head down and shake it slowly back and forth.

"I'm afraid she's chasing cats. She likes to tree them."

"Yep, that's what she does. We've been watching her do that to the weird lady's cat. She really gets mad."

I call out for Maya a few more times, but by now I have a following. Everywhere I walk, they traipse after me, not exactly in single file, more of a bunching together, vying for my attention. I kneel down, and the boys introduce themselves. I do a double take with Lionel and Otis. They are both so small and dirty that it takes me a minute to realize they are twins. Oscar, their older brother, proudly announces this fact.

David is the oldest and takes the lead. "I guess your dog's name is Maya. We call her Guard Dog or Hero."

"And why is that?"

"She saved Woody's life. Woody would tell you, but he doesn't talk yet. His real name is Willy, but it sounds like Woody when he says it."

"So how did Maya save Woody's life?"

All five boys circle me. David takes hold of Woody's hand and points to his shirt.

"See that rip. Well, a pit-bull was chasing him. Guard Dog chased him off."

Woody stared up at me and then pointed over at a tree where Maya had a Siamese cat treed. "My ero."

I nod slowly, knowing that Maya is a hunter, always getting into trouble. I feel somewhat guilty for having to bring her home. My neighbors think she is unsafe, and to cats she is death waiting to happen.

David reads my face and gives me a wise look. "She is special. What kind of a dog is she?"

Without thinking I say, "She is a mutt."

Oscar pipes in with his eyes wide open. "What is a mutt?'

I don't know how it happened, but suddenly I'm explaining how dogs come to be. How they combine with a mixture of dogs to become a mutt, and no two mutts are the same.

Lionel and Otis open and close their mouths. Our conversation gets stickier, and before I know it I'm explaining how twins happen.

David sums it up for everyone. "You take a little of the mom and a little of the dad, who took a little from their moms and dads, and then you have a dog."

I smile. "Yep, that is mostly what I said."

All the boys hold hands and start swinging them. David looks back at his house and then at me. "I think I get it now. My mom and dad didn't know."

I know it is time to go before I'm asked to explain religion or politics. I call out, "Guardian Dog, come."

On cue, Maya runs over to me, tongue hanging from exhaustion. After she slobbers on me and all the boys, I hook her up to her leash and head back home.

I can hear the kids chant. "Maya, our hero, Maya our guard dog."

I walk with my head held high, marveling at her transformation.

Mad Hatter

Costumes offer a sense of power. Hats make statements. This story explores magic and innocence through the eyes of those gifted with deep connections to what fills the heart.

I closed my eyes, half dreaming. "Tell me about his hat."

My sister knew what I was asking and began the description:

"I think it was chocolate brown, with a short crown. The brim slid forward easy over his brow and tapered back toward his neck with a lift. As if it floated on top of his head. I liked the way the crown pinched ever so slightly."

"Did any of his hair stick out?"

"Not much hair, I don't think. All I remember is his sideburns."

Sideburns make a statement. I wondered what he wanted to tell the world. It takes time to finesse hair so close to the face. Were they a distraction? Did he manicure his facial hair to compensate for no head hair?

"How did he smell?"

"Come on, I didn't get that close. Open your eyes, for god's sake. You can't tell anything by hats or smells. A man is more than that."

My sister thought she knew what she was talking about. Her boyfriend wore a ten-gallon hat. Its crown stood ten inches high with a center crease as wide as the Rio Grande. He even cinched his lanyard with a flashy bead that imitated gold. Whenever I looked at him, all I ever saw was ego. With his pointy leather boots, he stood over six feet tall. I suspect that without the hat, he'd be her size. His cologne gave him away, sickeningly sweet.

"Hats tell lots about a man, and so does his smell. I once knew a man who wore a beret. He'd cock it to the side and let the soft brim dance above his eye. He smelled like stale cigarettes and pot. His voice was kind when he read poetry, but he couldn't keep a thought."

My sister knew only cowboy hats. I'd been to the city, traveled across the ocean, where some men wore hats woven with straw, light and cool. They wore the hats not as adornments, but as protection from the scalding sun. A well-worn hat showed how prosperous a man was, how much land he had tilled and harvested.

"Just because you've traveled doesn't mean I don't know a thing or two. I suppose you'll start telling me about baseball caps and how men who wear them are fun-loving, or irresponsible, or childish. I think you are scared of hats. Get a life."

I had my life, and now I was faced with hats. I touched the top of my head and felt the bumps and lumps. A few wisps of hair remained. The strands reminded me of my long locks, which once cascaded down to my shoulders. I could still smell the sourness of my treatments.

Hats and turbans lined the walls of the room. Every country and small town was represented. My collection toured the world: Mexican sombreros, Panamanian straw hats, sailor and captain's caps, hats woven from the finest mohair, felt berets. I had learned to recreate them all. Surrounded by bolts of material, sewing machines, bindings, hatbands, bows, buttons, eyelets, beads, and straps, I worked from early morning until late at night. The room pressed the world inside. I wrote by hand the history of every hat I had created, my one small attempt to bridge cultures, to make the world a place of understanding.

The bells jingled, announcing the first customer of the day. My sister sat across from me, planted like a cactus, pricking me with her stare.

"Aren't you going to help the customer? It's your job."

"I quit."

"So this is your new ploy. Okay, you win. You're fired."

I had stopped greeting customers over a year ago, preferring to conserve my energy for my creative processes. My sister Mary would jump up any time she saw me tire, and rush to open the door. At first I protested, insisting that I had to size up the customers, get their aura, their unique karma, before I could take on a new commission. She countered my objections by saying I could observe from the back window. Watch and listen. She told me to trust her intuition. I did, and the hats I created were still beautiful. The customers never seemed to mind my absence and paid without complaint, but even Mary admitted that the hats lacked something. I knew what they lacked. They were no longer magical.

Scanning the bolts of material lying on the table, I found one of royal blue silk with gold threads running sporadically through the background. I cut off less than a yard and quickly wrapped it over and around my bald head. The excess trailed off behind me, making me look exotic and eccentric. Smiling with a false confidence, I entered the storefront with a straight back and hand extended, to face the voice calling from the front counter.

"Hello, anyone here? Hello."

"Hello to you. I'm Sarah. I'm sorry to have kept you waiting." My hand felt heavy extended, waiting for the other half of a handshake. I'm not sure where the awkwardness came from. I slipped my hand into my side pocket, and looked up at the face greeting me.

I can't say that the eyes sparkled or that the gentleman's smile caught my breath. I could only look at the skin around the chin and jaws, noting evidence of the outdoors. Lines where smiles once existed dipped into the folds of thickened cheeks. The edges of the lips teased upward, but were forced to remain flat, expressionless, mouthing words I couldn't hear.

"Excuse me, sir, I didn't catch your name."

"I guess I didn't offer it to you. I'm Jake to my friends."

"And who are you to your enemies?"

"Jake."

"Well, Jake, what can I help you with today?"

The silence hung so heavily in the air that I had to turn my head. It was as if Jake's life depended on his answer. I kept my back to him out of politeness and to ease my own discomfort. I should have been in the back room. I wasn't ready for people up close yet. My own skin prickled, my head itched under the turban, and my heart beat too steadily, reminding me that I was a survivor.

He groped for something in his front pocket. Pulling out a crumpled photograph, he cleared his throat and pointed. "Can you make me a hat like that?"

I reached for the photo to get a better look. For a second we struggled, my hand grasping the edge of the photo, his two hands clinging to the sides of what appeared to be all that he owned. I let my one free hand touch his wrist. The sensation jostled some emotion loose, and Jake finally released his hold.

The photo was of two people: an older man dressed in a suit with an informal, soft sportsman's felt hat, and a younger woman with a wider-brimmed version of the same type of soft felt. The two were holding hands, and a child climbed onto a car trying to sneak into the shot.

"Nope, I can't make you that hat."

Jake studied my face, looking to see if I was serious. He took the photo from my hand and started to turn away.

I could hear Mary in the back room coughing. She probably thought I was crazy. At least I knew it. I shouldn't be out here, raw with emotions and feeling stories. My patrons deserved more tact, more sensitivity. I blame the chemo for robbing me of finesse, my outer coating of charm killed along with the cancer. Chemotherapy destroys everything in its wake. The hair on my head was nothing but vanity, but even my eyelashes were gone, the hair on my arms and in the private areas. I no longer had a buffer of protection from the world, and I had no way of protecting the world from my illogical views and perceptions.

"I can make you what you need, but I can't make you that hat."

Jake's lips parted as if to talk. He moved his jaw back and forth, let the soft skin on his cheeks massage his words before he let them spill out. "Sarah, you have no manners. Good day."

As the door closed, Mary stomped into the front room.

"That went well."

"I've got work to do. Can you cover the front for about an hour?"

"I thought you were all caught up with your orders."

"I am. I'm going to make Jake the hat he needs."

"Sarah, what do you think you are doing? We

can't afford to work for free. Besides, you don't even know his last name, his phone number, or if he will ever set foot in this shop again."

"The little boy in the picture was Jake. His parents are lost to him. He wants them back. I'm not sure, but he regrets many losses, and the hat he wants isn't what he should be wearing."

"I shouldn't have let you come out to the front of the shop. Ever since you had cancer, you think you know about life. Not your own life, which by the way I think is disintegrating, but the life of everyone else. Maybe you are just a busybody, sticking your views onto others."

"I'm a hatter. That's all. I make hats, hats that suit the wearer, to nudge them along."

"I can cover the front for only an hour. I have an interview at eleven this morning."

So this was Mary's reason for getting me out into the shop. I had been selfish these last few months. All the time I was dealing with the lumps and illness, she had put her own life on hold. I felt contrite. I guess my sixth sense about others didn't extend to my own sister.

"Any place I know?"

"Not unless you go to a beauty parlor. I'm enrolling in cosmetology school and want to get some experience."

"Doing hair?"

Without thinking, my hand went up to touch my makeshift turban. I felt for the soft waves, the bounce that was once mine. Mary and I had cut my hair shorter and shorter as the months of treatment dragged on. Our theory had been to take control of the inevitable loss of locks and ease the shock of baldness.

"Nah—I'm not interested in hair. I want to be a makeup artist. I like to draw out people's personalities.

Stretch them to be all of what they can be."

I couldn't help but stifle my laugh. Mary never wore makeup. Her face was perfect: smooth skin, dark, defined eyebrows framing wide blue eyes. Before I said anything, I took another look. Sure enough, I had missed the liner, the soft blue shade on her eyelids. Even her lips glistened.

"So you think you have a talent for seeing a person's potential?"

"Sarah, you aren't the only one with a gift."

She was right. Although we were very different, Mary and I both knew from an early age that our relationships with others were unique. We often talked about it when we were kids, trying to fall asleep. Our talks might seem like gossip to others, but we always talked about what we imagined for our friends, never about what they did.

"I hope you get the job. Maybe you could work on me."

"Yeah, I could do a lot for you."

"Enough, I'm in the back, working on Jake's hat."

Already the twinges of Jake's life were passing through me. I hurried to my drawing table, clearing off the clutter of other work. I hooked a fresh sheet of tracing paper onto the tilted board, turned the miniature light on, and began. Images flashed in front of me. I had only seen Jake's photograph for less than a minute. The faces were less important than the positioning of the people. The older man was tall, the woman's head only reaching his shoulder as she leaned into him, depositing her thoughts, her worries, resting in a moment of release. The two held hands. Ironically, hers were the stronger of the two. Smaller, smoother, but more powerful, they emitted energy that the man clung to. Jake, in the background, tried to enter their field of commitment, lost in their devotion, their dedication, their ease of sharing.

My hand shook as I began to sketch. I couldn't discern if the chemo had robbed me of sensations, or if the sensations I was feeling were so intense that the lines wavered. My first image was of a plastic fireman's hat, the next of a stocking cap: hot and cold, fire and ice. I saw flames streaming out of a house, a snowman, and a fort with snowballs lined, ready for battle.

I drew circle after circle, round packed snow, not too icy, not too mushy. I filled the page with spheres except for one corner. There Jake stood small with his right hand raised up and behind his head, the trajectory of the snowball hitting a second-story window on the house. Flames curled out the lip of the window. Jake threw faster, harder, trying to knock the flames down. The fumes overwhelmed me. I could smell the smoke as if I were inside the picture. Each breath brought the smoke into my damaged lungs, piercing the spots where cancer had already raged.

I had to close my eyes. Take a break from the heat. It felt like my radiation treatments. My heart hurt. I clutched my chest. At least I still had my two breasts. No one could see the ravaging of my insides. The counseling sessions for cancer survivors never mention how close the lungs are to the heart. They fail to tell us that the treatments make your heart work harder, make you feel life more intensely. As if I hadn't felt life intensely before.

The grandfather clock in the front of the store bonged eleven times. Mary appeared by my work bench.

"I have to go. I'm late already."

"I'm not keeping you."

"You look like you just came from one of your treatments. What happened?"

I pointed to my drawings and shrugged. "Just another one of my emotional preliminary hat exercises."

Mary studied the pictures I had drawn. Her finger lingered on the second-story window. As she walked out the door, she mumbled, "Find out who is inside that room."

"Don't just leave, throwing me your insight. What makes you think someone was inside that room?"

"Oh, I forgot to mention that Jake came back while you were working. I thought you would have heard us talking."

"You know that I'm oblivious to anything when I'm working."

Mary pursed her lips, dismayed, but I saw the twinkle shine through her eyelashes, what I called her smiling eyes. I loved the way she knew me. I depended on her understanding to function.

"A horrible habit I hope I will not have to cope with the rest of my life."

Clutching my heart, I whined, "You have wounded me." And she had. We knew each other too well. I was the more independent one, the traveler, the initiator. Yet Mary had always been there to support me and guide me when my obsessions took over. I sensed that she wanted to be free of me. More precisely, she wanted to be more with herself.

"Go, you're late for your interview. I'll go out front now, and work on Jake's hat later tonight."

I expected a futile reprimand, cautioning me on the virtues of paying customers. Instead Mary countered, "He wants his hat next week. He told me to tell you, and I quote, "Tell Sarah that I want a hat, one that matches her fiery personality and that will suit my needs."

I raced after Mary as she went out the front door. "Did he leave the photograph?"

"Look on the counter."

I ducked back inside the door and headed for the counter. The ringing of bells followed as three small children walked in with a bedraggled mother. Her request was simple. She wanted four matching bonnets, the old-fashioned kind that tied under the chin and billowed out around the face. "We're in the Easter parade that begins at the church. I don't have money for new dresses, and I thought maybe new hats would help us celebrate."

Already I was mentally scanning my choices of material, ribbons, and ties. I noted the faces of the three girls. Each had a hopeful, open smile. The oldest held my eyes. Hers were emerald green ovals with small flecks of brown. She walked up to the counter and gave me her hand. I touched the soft pads of skin, baby flesh not yet spoiled by the wear and tear of life's demands. She could be no more than six, but she held me transfixed, drawing me into her spell. Her eyes and hands created a cooling effect. I felt it in her palms, her stare fanning my burning lungs and heart.

"Is there something special you want on your bonnet?"

"Yes, please. Could you make it so my mommy smiles? She likes flowers and birds and anything beautiful because they are alive."

What had happened in their household for this child to know the insides of her mother's heart? All she wanted was her mom to smile with life. A tall order I wasn't sure my bonnets could fill.

"Do you know what flower is your mother's favorite?"

"Shh, this is my surprise. Don't make them daisies. She cries when she sees daisies. Make them rosebuds."

I nodded and finished writing up the order. Her mother seemed oblivious to our conversation. We agreed on a date and a price that would make my sister Mary wince.

Just as I was ushering the family out, my newfound friend took my hand and pointed to the picture Jake had left on the counter.

"Those girls never got to wear an Easter bonnet. It was too hot."

Confused, I grabbed the photo. It wasn't the one Jake had been holding of his parents. Instead, he had left me a picture of two little girls with pigtails, dressed in old-fashioned play suits, one-piece striped jumpsuits with elastic around the bathing suit bottoms connected to halter tops with ties around the neck. I had worn a similar summer outfit when I was five.

The little girl holding my hand had tears in her eyes. I bent down and kissed her cheek.

"Thanks for letting me know. I'll do my best for them as well. You better catch up with your mother, or she'll be worried."

"Bye. Stay cool."

Her gentle touch had cooled me down considerably, but her insights disturbed me. Observant and caring, she reminded me of myself. Just for a moment I let myself imagine my own future child at six.

∞

The rest of the day passed without any real demands. The few new hats commissioned were for old customers whose needs were less taxing. They all greeted me as if I hadn't disappeared for eight months, and only a handful had asked for Mary. For my first day back, I hadn't done so badly. Still, I wasn't ready to man the store alone. I secretly hoped that Mary's interview went poorly.

She found me in the midst of strewn, crumpled paper, bolts of red, yellow, lavender, and coral material, with my hands tangled in a mess of pipe cleaners. Transfixed with mental images of flames, windows, and the eyes of innocent children, I fashioned a border of roses as decorative trim.

"Sarah, do you know what time it is?" She placed her hands on my shoulders and shook me gently. "Sarah, I'm talking to you. Can you stop for just a minute and be of this world?"

"Mmmm, while you are holding my shoulders, could you massage my neck?"

"I don't know why I even bother, you are hopeless. It is close to nine o'clock, and I'm sure you haven't eaten dinner."

"What did you bring me?"

"A piece of my mind. If I hadn't dropped by, you'd be up all night working without food or sleep."

I had expected Mary to return earlier. Ignoring my hunger, I had delved into the picture Jake left. I became the five-year-old of this morning's encounter, saw with her eyes, and felt with her heart. The images merged so that I could no longer distinguish between the Easter bonnets for her family and the hat Jake had requisitioned. The two girls in the window... were so hot. I needed to make five hats, and all I could think of was roses.

I eyed Mary to see if her irritation stretched beyond her words. She had changed from this morning into a pair of jeans and a flannel shirt. Looking relaxed and refreshed, she had washed off her makeup, and her face shone like a fresh peach. I took this as a good sign.

"How did your interview go?"

"I wondered if you'd even remember."

"Come on, I'm not that insensitive. Once you beat me over the head a few times, I respond. So did the beauty parlor hire you?"

"They loved me. But if they knew you were my sister, they would never have hired me."

I dropped the rose-formed pipe cleaners on the counter and closed my eyes. Usually I'm not sensitive to Mary's slights. She often talks in opposites, a backward way of complimenting me, but for some reason her jibe hit me in my heart. Tears formed and coated the rims of my eyes so that when I opened them, I saw a rainbow of colors through the light. I knew immediately what had happened to Jake's sisters.

"Sarah, I'm sorry. I didn't mean to hurt your feelings. You did too much today. It's late, and I know you haven't eaten. I'll cook you something at our house."

Words refused to form on my lips. They felt parched, dry and burnt, as if I had been leaning against a window heated by the noon sun.

∞

Monday came too quickly. Mary was off with her cowboy lover, gallivanting through the countryside, and I passed the weekend fretting about the tragedy and loss of complete strangers. I took long walks and gathered rose hips from the hedges of wild roses that bordered our house. I walked in fields where paintbrush dotted the hills, emerging from the burnt remains of a languishing forest. Orange, yellow, and red petals punctuated unspoken thoughts of Jake. He had crept inside my exposed head, lay under the thin skin that covered my thoughts.

Working at a feverish pace, I had finished four Easter bonnets. I pressed the rose hips into the pipe cleaner molds I had fashioned and wove a garland of hope to surround each of the rounded crowns. Using a combination of felt and material, I transformed the bonnets into headdresses that had form and no form, allowing structure and spontaneity to coexist. The crown held tight to the thoughts and feelings of the mother, and the brim fell softly and whimsically, allowing the children to grow into their lives. The emerald eyes of the oldest daughter dictated the bonnet's color. A hummingbird appeared at intervals, flitting around each head, carrying the sweet nectar of pale, pink roses and white lilies. You could almost smell the mesmerizing fragrance of grace, gentility, and refinement. Mingled in among the flowers, orange and yellow roses unfurled at half-mast, the warmth of orange declaring pride and the yellow suppressing jealousy. I had tried to stay clear of the mother's sadness evoked by daisies. I worried more about the jealousy she felt and the undeveloped pride in her brood.

With the bonnets done, I was free to work on Jake's hat. Free isn't exactly what I felt.

Mary bounced into the shop humming some godawful country tune.

"How can you sing so early in the morning?

"I see you had a fine weekend. In case you wondered, I eloped this weekend and am happily married."

I looked sideways, not wanting to believe her. She had to be joking about marriage. We had never talked about this or her job aspirations. I felt cold, as if the heat from my heart was leaking out of my head.

I took the high road and said what I didn't feel.

"It's about time that man made you legitimate. I hated having a sister living in sin. The town has been aghast at your behavior."

Mary burst out in laughter. I expected her to see through my ruse, but instead she just held me in a sisterly bear hug. "I knew you'd be happy for me. I feel like my life is a waterfall, cascading at uncontrollable speed. I guess it was the snow this winter melting."

All I noticed was that since last week, nothing would be the same. Even the cancer hadn't altered my life to this extent. I was losing a sister, a partner, and a friend. Mary would no longer be at the shop, no longer have the time to watch out for me or share my thoughts. The coldness I felt on the outside was nothing compared to the heat burning my lungs, boiling inside.

I could feel the fire in the burning house, the panic of the little girls watching their parents, not able to leave. I knew then that Jake was born after their death and could never change the outcome. His parents loved him, but never in the same way as his sisters. They didn't dare to. It was too risky. No matter what Jake did, he couldn't put out the flames of sadness. He had turned cold. The picture he had showed me was of his parents' total devotion to themselves. The picture he left behind was the ache of longing.

I heard the jiggling of the front door, knew without looking that Jake was outside waiting to get in. The store wasn't to open for another hour. Mary turned her back to the store, so I had no choice but to answer the ringing bell.

"Thought you wouldn't be here this early."

"Then why'd you come?"

"Are you going to let me in or what?"

"I guess I'll do the what, and come outside."

I closed the door behind me and stood outside

the store with Jake. Neither of us knew what to do. I had come out without a scarf. I was barer than being naked. Jake wasn't polite enough not to stare. He took his time looking at me. I'm not sure what he saw, but I know what I saw reflected back. The folds of skin around his cheeks and jaw filled out into a recognizable smile. His eyes softened, and the green of the pastures and fields where I had meandered over the weekend became him. Even after a horrible forest fire, plants resurface, as I had witnessed with the blossoming paint-brush. Jake's face glowed, a warm golden-orange as if kissed by the sun.

We walked awkwardly along the empty sidewalks. He had changed positions with me, acting the gentleman, taking the outside. I wished he had spared me this courtesy. I hated seeing my own reflection in the stores' windows. I focused on the spacing between each pavement slab. I took three steps to Jake's two. We found a rhythm, and gradually the tension between us eased.

"Do you ever say good morning to anyone?"

I looked up slowly and tried to judge if Jake was challenging me. His voice, soft and questioning, only revealed the question as a question. He didn't mean anything by it.

"Well, I usually don't have the opportunity to say good morning, as I live alone and I work mostly in the back of the store, sewing. I guess I've been rude."

"The thought had crossed my mind, but with your explanation, I just think you're rusty."

I couldn't help but smile—rusty was an understatement. I'd been out of circulation for a few years. Whatever I used to know about social skills and wooing a suitor had covered me with a flaky coating of irritability. If Jake's face glowed golden, mine glowered burnt brown.

"Let me try again. Good morning, Jake, whoever you are, what can I help you with?"

Jake's body shook and his laugh filled the street. I refused to be embarrassed. He had asked for a proper greeting.

"My dog greets me better, but I won't make you try again. I wanted to know if you were going to make me a hat. I don't know why I couldn't give you the picture of my parents."

His voice got quieter and his words came out fast, so that I could barely catch what he was saying.

"I didn't want to let go of them, to give up. Did your sister give you the one I left the other day?"

"The picture of the two girls, your sisters, was more important anyway. You gave me what I needed to make you a hat. So the answer is yes. The hat will be done by the end of the week."

"That soon?"

I stood still and turned to look at Jake. He hadn't realized that I had called the girls his sisters, that I knew the story of their death. He was clueless, yet clung to me for some divine revelation.

"Jake, I make hats. I don't create miracles. Under the right circumstances I can make a hat in a week. Did you want me to take more time, so you could hold onto your anguish longer?"

"There you go again, Sarah, getting snippety. Did you know that sarcasm is a device for hiding, that it is hurtful, and not at all attractive?"

"What makes you so sure that I want to be attractive?"

"Oh, you already are attractive, you're just trying hard to turn anybody away that might think you are."

He got me on that one. I was the only person I needed to convince of anything. For the life of me,

I didn't know why Jake got under my skin. Maybe I reacted because he was reading me. Couldn't he find a book instead, something complete with a beginning, middle, and an end?

Without thinking, I reached my hand up to touch his face. Reflexively Jake moved his head to the side, as if warding off a blow, and grabbed my wrist. I didn't resist. We stood on the sidewalk in front of my store almost holding hands. I could feel the sun warming my head and face, gathering moisture along my lips.

"I was only going to touch your face, feel your skin so I could find out more about you. I didn't mean to startle you."

"You do that to all of your hat customers?"

This time it was my turn to laugh. Suddenly the day felt light and airy. I had just dished out a line. Even if there was some truth to what I had said, I knew that I wanted to feel more, that despite my intuitiveness, my ability to see into my customers, I was behaving like a crazed female. I thought of my sister apparently so enamored with love that she had eloped over the weekend. I didn't know whether to feel ridiculous or to just accept that I was human.

"Jake, I have to go back to work. The store opens in a few minutes."

Ever so gently, he placed my hand over his mouth. I felt his chin move slightly upward, his lips gather and part as the whisper of a "Shh" warmed my palm. Letting go, he saluted me.

"Should I stop by in a week?'

Before I could answer, I spotted my little Easter bonnet friend across the street trailing behind her sisters and mother. She waved frantically. I shuddered as I watched her run across the street without looking. Apparently Jake noticed her as well and ran into the street just as a cyclist raced by. In one sweep of his arms he had scooped her up and deposited her by my feet.

I knelt down beside her and opened my arms. She slipped inside as if she belonged.

"Shh… Don't say anything for a minute. I know you want to yell at me 'cause I ran across the street without looking. My mom always waits and counts to ten. Then you can just tell me I was wrong and not yell."

I did as I was told, marveling as I counted at her ability to use and articulate her mother's wisdom. After I arrived at the number ten, I released her from my embrace. "What was so important that you would forget the rules and be careless like that?"

"I needed to tell you something about him."

She pointed at Jake, who was still standing on the sidewalk like a soldier protecting his troops. His eyes were moist, fixed on us. His lips trembled.

"Whatever you have to say, you need to spill it out quickly. Your mother is pacing across the street, calling out your name. Yolanda suits you well."

"She calls me Yolanda when she is angry with me. Yoyo is my name when I'm being good."

"Quickly, Yoyo, we have to get you back to her. What is it about Jake you want to tell me?"

"His heart is burning. He has to turn it down but not off. You might get burned too."

Yoyo didn't wait for my reaction. She looked both ways, saw no cars and walked across the street as if her message was a simple statement, not the riddle that caused both Jake and me to gasp.

Jake waited until Yoyo was back with her Mom before he turned to face me.

"Next week. I'll pick up the hat."

I nodded. "Be careful."

"As a trained firefighter, I always am."

∞

Mary had already counted the till, pulled up the shades, and turned on the open sign by the time I walked back inside my shop.

I meant to congratulate her for real, say the appropriate thing to a newlywed, but I was distracted. Whatever I had been feeling toward Jake was altered by Yoyo's statement. So he was a fireman. That made sense. Subconsciously he was trying to rescue his two sisters who died in a fire. But Yoyo's statement changed that.

Instead of saying anything, I placed a freshly steamed Chai latte on the counter. Mary acknowledged my presence by taking a sip and nodding my way. Ah, yes, there was nothing like the comfort of silence. I loved how we could always depend on understanding or misunderstanding and continuing to enjoy each other's habits. I watched Mary as she hummed her way into the day. She was dancing inside to a tune of contentment.

I, on the other hand, had awakened a girlish flittering of emotions inside. It felt more like the jitterbug than the salsa. The only way to calm the fiery nerves was to rearrange the finished hats displayed on the walls. This, too, had been Mary's idea. One evening she stayed late hammering wide-angled hooks into the wall. By the next morning the entire room was transformed with fuchsia, violet, emerald, and ocean blue ensembles to entice walk-in customers. All these hats were half done, waiting only for a customer to decide on their own flair. These hats were for the walk-in customers who just wanted to spend money. They were fashion-conscious, people who had most of what they needed, and didn't need my talents of discovery.

I took each one down from its perch, dusted it

and placed it over my own crown. Thirty hats to keep in shape, an impressive show of normalcy. I stood in front of the mirror pretending I was a customer. With patience and hope I tried to envision each as my own. I caught Mary staring at me with a smirk on her face.

"What is so funny? Can't I try on my own hats? The only way I can tell if they are keeping their proper form is to try them on."

"Who are you trying to fool? Certainly not me. None of those hats are for you. You are in one of your searching moods again. What did Jake want that set you off? Whatever it was, you're acting like a hummingbird, twittering around in search of something sweet."

"He was just asking about when his hat would be ready. I told him next week, which seemed to surprise him. I don't know about him. Something isn't quite right. Remember that little girl whose mom wanted those Easter bonnets? She ran across the street to warn me about Jake. Something about turning the fire down so I wouldn't get burned."

I could hear the breath slowly leave Mary's mouth. One of her deeper sighs of exasperation at my comments.

"Was it a warning? Sometimes you read too much into people's actions. The little girl is only about six. More than likely she saw you with Jake and observed you two making eyes at each other. Could be that's the burning she referred to."

Now it was my turn to be exasperated. I walked quietly to the back of the store, sat down at my table, and pulled out Jake's hat. I had cut out the design first in a stiff gauze material. Today I would pick the felt from my special collection and stretch it over a styrofoam head of his size. This part was the most difficult. I was from the old school, making the felt from beaver and rabbit fur. Each year I passed weeks treating the furs with a solution similar to mercury, then shaving off the skin and immersing the fibers in a boiling acid to thicken and harden. For Jake's hat I wanted to use beaver felt. The brown felt square was silky smooth to my touch. I took a large iron, filled it with water, and let the steam soften the felt, then molded it to the styrofoam. Beads of sweat circled the crown of my head, curling under my turban. The fumes made me somewhat dizzy.

Before I knew it, I heard a timer go off, Mary's newest trick to bring me back to a more scheduled life. Whenever I got absorbed in a project, she would set the timer for one hour. She felt that I could compartmentalize my creative juices and then be ready to face the public. It was her push for my balance. Ever since I had had radiation, Mary felt that my behavior was too eccentric. She complained that I was slipping away, either raging on some emotion or hiding motionless.

"Are you angry with me, Sarah? I hate it when you disappear after I've said something profound."

"You cheated. That wasn't an hour. You could have at least given me an hour to work."

"Not when I know you are avoiding me."

This is exactly why I loved Mary. She knew I couldn't hide. And that is precisely why I was angry at her.

I put Jake's hat on my own bald head and let the brim cover my eyes. The netting allowed the air to flow through and cool my thoughts. Anger was my escape from loss. It was always easier to fume rather than risk caring. Jake's hat floated over me, swirling an energy that blew anger away. Slipping into a semi-trance, I kept my eyes open, watching as the mist evaporated. Darkness lifted to so much green. I saw single blades of grass, pine needles, maidenhair soft and willowy with black fine lines of connection. Focusing on the featherlike maidenhair ferns, I felt the breezes of life tug and pull, but the filament held each leaf intact. I was in the center of green, holding on, fragile like the maidenhair but still tethered.

Mary pulled Jake's hat upward, exposing my eyes. She smiled her mischievous smile.

"Peek-a-boo, I see you."

"You always could, even when I was hiding."

"What did you discover inside of Jake's hat? What did it tell you?"

Placing it back on the foam head, I shook my own. "Nothing about Jake. His presence wasn't there. I could feel a pale green surge of hope mixed with the fearful pull of loss. Whatever it means, I don't want to let go."

Mary gave me a bear hug that had me sputtering for breath.

"Let me go, I can't breathe."

"What did you say? I can't understand you. First you want me to hold on, keep you safe, now you want me to let you go."

I gave up struggling, and as soon as I did, Mary let go. I collapsed in the rocking chair set out for waiting customers.

"I'm not going to say I'm sorry that I eloped or that I have a new job. I'm not letting you go."

I let my lips turn upside down in a familiar pout, but just like when we were young, after one look at Mary making silly faces, they had nowhere to go but upward.

"So, when will you and your cowboy have kids? I can't wait to be an auntie."

Shooing me away with her hand, Mary stammered, "Whoa, Sarah, I've got work to do. Why don't you sew and design awhile? I'll take care of the front till lunch. Then you are on. Kids are not something I choose to talk about."

I walked slowly back to my design table. I had failed to tell Mary that I had seen Yolanda's eyes inside the green imagery of Jake's hat. She was invisible, but her eyes spoke to that fragile maidenhair, the thread that held me dangling. Mary had to be right, that her warning was just a childish awareness of sensual energies. I wondered when and where I had lost that ability to sense things in their innocence.

Mary and I never talked about our childhood any more. We didn't need to, since we were each other's best friend and had lived our childhood together. The loss of our parents left us to fend for ourselves. I wondered if her marriage would change my best friend status and leave me to fend for myself. I couldn't afford to lose the only person who really understood me.

Jake still had his parents, but he was alone, haunted by a memory that didn't include him. And Yoyo, she knew too much for a kid, the oldest of the brood, watching out for the mom.

I sewed by hand, stitching the inside band with a soft, absorbent cloth. A material that would be thin enough for Jake not to notice, but would also catch his sweat before it dripped into his face. This hat would be worn always and forever. It was to be his topping, his protection, and the cover that kept him from disappearing into the sky above.

∞

By lunch time, I was ravenous. I didn't need the timer to bring me back to the world as my stomach growled its signal. I emerged into the shop expecting Mary to be walking out the door. Instead, she was holding court. Yoyo and her family posed in front of the mirrors wearing their Easter bonnets. Yoyo's mom stood transfixed. Her eyes, no longer empty, sparkled green, fertile with life. Whatever her worries had been, she seemed at ease. She smiled a thank you to me as she held her three girls in front of her. Yoyo was tugging at her skirt and looking my way. I wondered, if I were ever to have a child, would she be as precocious as Yoyo?

"Yoyo, you and your sisters look almost as beautiful as your mom. I hope you like your bonnets."

Yoyo's two sisters stood behind her, peeking out to see me while they giggled. Yoyo was their voice and protector. "We love them. Thank you for the roses. These are happy hats. You should have a happy hat like ours."

"I should, should I? I'll have to design one with roses, too. But today I'm wearing a pink turban."

One of Yoyo's sisters whispered something, and Yoyo gave her a steely look.

"What did your sister want?"

"She wanted to see what was under your turban."

I could feel my face turn crimson and tears well up in the corner of my eyes. I forced myself to smile. I knelt down close to Yoyo and her sisters and slowly unraveled my turban. I didn't want to frighten them. I didn't want to frighten myself.

"My hair fell out after my cancer treatments. It is taking a very long time to grow back."

Their eyes widened, their lips formed a circle, and I heard a soft, "Oohhhhh."

Yoyo stepped forward and placed her hand on my head. Her sisters broke formation and rushed to touch the top of my head. Their fingers brushed over my stubbles, creating static, sending little waves of electricity through me. They stood encircling me with broad smiles. Peals of laughter rang out. Mine came from my belly, rising through my heart and breathlessly through my lungs. The girls danced in delight.

I finally stood up when I realized their mother was standing there waiting. I shooed them out.

"Off you go, girls, have fun at the parade."

They rushed for the door with their mom in the lead. The music from "When the Saints Come Marching In" trickled in. You could feel the rhythms of excitement in the air.

The store felt emptier with their absence, but the hushed quiet that remained contained sparks of their spirit. I felt unsettled and queasy inside. Slowly I rewrapped the turban around my head. I took time to knot the front into the shape of a flower, allowing the multi-colors of the fabric to create the illusion of a garden.

Mary came up behind me and squeezed my shoulders.

"Are you okay, Sarah?"

"I don't know. I sometimes wonder if I am becoming the Mad Hatter. Remember the scene in *Alice in Wonderland,* when Alice says to the Cat that she doesn't want to be among mad people? The Cat told her that she couldn't help that because we were all mad. I just wonder if I am madder than insightful."

"Are you asking me, if you are crazy?"

"Not exactly, but yes, that is what I'm afraid of. I want to blame the cancer treatments for my oversensitivity, but I wonder about hatters in general. Hatters really did go mad in the past because of their overexposure to mercury. They would slowly lose their memory, have distorted vision, and develop hallucinations."

"Are you hallucinating?"

"No, at least I don't think so. I always thought of my intuitions about people as being a gift, but lately I miss what is before my eyes. I worry that my visions are really a too-active imagination. I worry that I've crossed the line."

"What line is that?"

"Oh, you know the one where they take you away, put you in a straitjacket."

"Come on, if they ever put you in a straitjacket you'd have to decorate it with sparkles, and the next thing they would be designer straitjackets, selling at top price to all the movie stars. We'd be rich and famous."

"I'd settle for just rich."

"If rich was your goal, you'd have charged more for those Easter bonnets."

Apparently I hadn't gotten away with anything. Mary caught my special pricing, a system I had perfected by calculating need times ability-to-pay, with need weighing more in the formula. My math teacher would call it a negative ratio system. I just shrugged and gave Mary my charming grin.

I turned the Open sign to Closed, placed my arm inside of Mary's bent elbow, and walked down the street toward the Easter Parade. Already the smells of hot dogs, popcorn, and fried apple fritters lured me on. Mary went for the hot dog, and I found myself biting into the crunchiest and sweetest apple fritter in existence. The white powdered sugar lingered on my lips.

Mary's husband was the parade's organizer, and I spotted him in the front of all the floats, clad in a long black cape and silk top hat. The Mad Hatter himself. Before I could comment on the irony of his costume, Mary was off running to meet him.

I shouted after her, "Don't fall through the rabbit hole."

Laughing, she shouted back, "Don't disappear on me. I'll meet you back at the store."

Within seconds the crowd swallowed her. My arms dangled beside me, heavier without Mary's touch. Through the swarm of bright blue, green, yellow, and pink dresses, white baskets, little kids dressed as bunnies with floppy ears, I meandered to the last pausing spot of the parade. I liked watching from the backseat, letting the momentum of the parade gain energy. My store was only three blocks away, but the festivities of the parade transported me faraway into another time frame, another existence. I was back in my childhood on the same street, walking down the center of the parade. Dressed as a fairy godmother, I waved my wand at the crowd, granting their wishes.

Even in my adult body I felt the magic of spring, the awe of a child. I could have been Yoyo's best friend at the age of six. Yoyo's infectious smile was inside me. I conjured up her family and surprised myself when I saw the rose hips of their Easter bonnets crowded in among the lines of people waiting at the edge of the sidewalk.

Yoyo held her Easter basket in close. Instead of facing the road and watching the fanfare of the marching bands, the juggling clowns, the spray of confetti, she was facing the houses and lawns set back from the road. Every few feet she reached into her basket and then sprinkled the air. At first I thought she must be sprinkling fairy dust or some magical imagined potion, something I would have done years ago. I made my way closer and stepped in beside her.

"Hi, Yoyo. I spotted you and your family across the way and couldn't resist coming over. No one can miss you with those Easter hats. Are you having fun?"

I expected a hug or a smile at least, some childlike greeting. Instead Yoyo gave me a nod and brought her free hand to her mouth, signaling me to be quiet. I watched as she sprinkled seeds up and down the edge of the lawns. She had roamed away from her sisters and mother, and once again I felt the need to oversee her actions. I didn't want her to run out in the street as she had done that morning I had been walking with Jake. Finally, after an entire block was seeded, she looked up with a big grin.

"Want to know what I was doing?"

"I was hoping you would tell me."

"I'm making the world beautiful."

It was such a simple statement that it took my breath away.

"My mother read me a book from the library. She told me it takes sadness away if you try to make the world more beautiful daily. I'm planting lupines like the girl did in the story."

I bent down and kissed the top of Yolanda's head and took her hand. Despite the rosehips surrounding her bonnet, her hair smelled like ashes, and her hands were hot. Puzzled, I walked her back to her family, who hadn't quite missed her yet.

"Why did you pick this street?"

"I didn't pick the street. It picked me. I could feel heat coming from a house, a dark smell."

I squeezed Yolanda's hand and closed my eyes. The dark smell of smoke, the ashy smell from her hair. Her fingers were entwined in mine, and between each one a burning sensation emanated. Her palms were cool. At that moment, I felt what she did. Call it intuition, a psychic feeling, or madness, but I too knew that something bad was going to happen. I felt nauseated with fear, an inner heat, as if I had had another radiation treatment.

The last of the floats arrived just as we nestled in next to Yolanda's sisters and mother. Each of the kids smiled at me, acting as if it was the most normal thing in the world to see me at the parade. Kids take coincidences as the norm.

I no longer knew what normal was and tried to quiet my fears. Yolanda seemed to have forgotten all about the house.

I heard a siren in the distance and then the progressively louder blaring as a fire engine approached. I hadn't remembered Jake saying anything about the Fire Department being in the parade. But sure enough, kids hung from the sides of the truck, dressed as miniature firemen, throwing candy out to the crowd. Actual firemen fully clothed in their protective gear walked alongside the truck, smiling and waving. With each toot of the siren, candy flew into the air. Yolanda's sisters ran out onto the streets gathering loot with the other children.

Yoyo squirmed and squeezed my hand. Hers was burning up. And then I smelled it. The sulfur smell of smoke hit me, and I turned to see the last house on the road with smoke seeping out of the windows and chimney. Yolanda and I had only minutes before been at its doorsteps.

I wanted to flag down the fire truck that had just passed in the parade, make it stop. Instead of stopping, it drove slowly down the center of the road, ignoring the smoke-riddled house and rounding the corner. The sirens acted as a magnet, drawing the crowds and kids to follow. Yolanda held my hand tightly. I stood frozen in place, wondering if anyone was inside the house, wondering how the fire truck was going to get back to help, with the entire parade in pursuit.

I let go of Yolanda's hand, retrieved my cell phone from my pants pocket, and dialed 911.

"Hello, this is Sarah from the Hat Shop. There is a house in flames at the end of the parade on Elm Street. The fire truck was in the parade and it drove by without stopping."

"Don't worry, we're sending another unit out. We got a call not two minutes ago. Stay calm, you need to get everyone away from the road so the truck can get in."

Yoyo acted before me. It was as if she read my mind. She ran to the edge of the sidewalk where the red cones were lined up. Together we grabbed them and created a circular barrier in front of the houses.

By now the smoke had changed from a faint gray to a dark, billowing mass. From the top window, flames licked the air. I prayed that no one was inside, but my stomach told me otherwise. Yoyo stood facing the top window, pointing.

"Do you see them, Sarah? Do you see the two girls standing in the window?"

I heard more sirens coming from the other side of town. An eternity passed as I stared upward. I couldn't tell if my eyes and mind were playing tricks on me. Were there two young children standing in the window? I couldn't tell if the memory of Jake's sisters perishing in a fire colored my vision or if this was my own vision.

"I can't tell, Yoyo. The smoke is too thick. It might be shadows."

"No, I'm sure. We have to get them out."

"That isn't our job. The firemen will come. We have to stay safe and make sure that you get back to your mom and sisters."

Two fire engines and a ladder truck pulled up alongside the now-empty road. An ambulance drove over the sidewalk and parked to the side. The fire truck that had been in the parade barricaded the side street. Everyone from the parade remained away, all but Yoyo and me.

I didn't recognize anyone with the heavy coats and helmets, but I hoped that Jake was nearby. My skin prickled from heat. Two firemen jumped out of the first truck and immediately took the fire hose toward the house. The other truck hooked one hose up to the hydrant and another to the pump truck. It all seemed like a choreographed scene.

I heard Jake's voice before I spotted him. He was in command, directing a fireman to circle around the house, another fireman to place the ladder alongside the upstairs attic. Before I could stop her, Yolanda rushed toward the sound of his voice. She was tugging at his pant leg when I reached her.

Jake's face stiffened as his stare bore down on us.

"Sarah, why are you here? You have to get Yolanda away from the area."

I tried to scoop Yolanda up, remove her grip on Jake's pant leg. She held tight.

"Yolanda, let go of Jake's pants. He wants us to move away from the fire."

"Not until I tell him."

Jake kept looking beyond me, studying the scene, listening to his radio. He bent down to Yolanda.

"What do you need to tell me?"

"I saw them. I saw them in the window."

I was afraid that Jake wouldn't believe Yolanda. That he would ignore the urgency and go about his routine. Instead, Jake scooped her up in his arms, pulled his red helmet to the back of his head, and whispered ever so gently.

"Don't worry. I'll find them. What window, and who did you see?"

"There were two girls standing in the window. One was taller than the other. The smoke was everywhere. They were like ghosts waving at me. I saw them in the window next to your big ladder."

All three of us looked up at the window. Only smoke, dark gray filled the frame. My stomach muscles tightened, and I instinctively reached for Jake's arm to steady me. A rush passed through me as if Yoyo, Jake, and I somehow were one. I clearly saw the wave of a hand, the silhouette of two girls staring out at us.

"Come with me. I have to get you both out of the way."

I held onto his arm while he held Yolanda in close to his coat. I barely saw the crowds of people staring. Dazed, all I could manage was to move my feet one at a time alongside Jake. Nausea had set in with the vision of the girls.

"Jake, we can make our way. Go find the girls."

"From the look on your face, you can barely move. You've got a grip on my arm that doesn't lie. Besides, I've sent my crew in to scout each room. They make their way up each floor. They're good. They won't miss anyone, and if need be, I'll come in from behind."

"Are you being nice?"

"I'm doing my job. You and Yolanda are in my way. I want you to stay put inside the cab of the fire truck."

"Mary will worry, and so will Yolanda's Mom. We can't stay here."

"You can and will stay put. It isn't a request. It's an order."

Jake's face was hard. As he put Yolanda in

the back seat of the cab, he kept his gaze on me. He was willing me to stay put, warning me to behave. I wondered how he could read me, know I had no control over my intuitions. I nodded, fearing what I would say, and prayed that I wouldn't see images, feel compelled to move.

The smoke billowed darker, and flames licked the siding. I kept my eyes fixed on the top window. No one appeared. Yoyo had given up, and her head rested on my lap. I breathed with her breaths, trying to slow my heart to keep me in the moment. I couldn't afford a vision, yet I wanted more than anything to divide myself in two—no, three.

Perhaps that was my problem, scattering my energy in the past, propelling myself into the future, and fidgeting with apprehension in the present. I closed my eyes to conjure up my sister's face. I hoped she was tuned into our special wavelength of communication. She had to know I was safe. All I felt was static, the crackling of the fire, frantic fears old and new. I listened for Yolanda's breath, in out, in, in out, in out, out in. She must be dreaming.

It took a few seconds for me to recognize the beeping sound coming from my vibrating pocket. I flipped my cell phone open to hear Mary's frenzied voice.

"Are you okay? You disappeared into the smoke. What are you doing? Yolanda is missing. Tell me you have her."

"We're both fine. She's is sleeping in my lap."

"In your lap? Where is your lap?"

Even at the most intense times, Mary could make me smile.

"My lap is seated in the cab of the Jake's fire truck. Jake put us here to keep us out of his way. He's going to search for the two girls we saw in the house."

Mary's silence at the other end of the call sent a chill up my spine. I thought we had been disconnected. The chill triggered the vision I hadn't wanted to see: A red and blue glowing beam cracked, falling from the attic ceiling, dropping toward a huddled group of people.

"Sarah, are you sure you saw two people in the window? No one lives in that house. It belonged to the Hendricks, who moved last month. Remember, you made them hats."

My thoughts ping-ponged inside my head. The house was empty, there were two people inside, the owners moved away, there was a fire at an empty house where no one lived and two people were trapped. No matter how I twisted the facts, they didn't add up to anything that made sense. Yolanda's head dug deeper into my thigh, she turned fitfully, and I felt a tear drop on my pants.

My sister's voice broke into my attempt to rake through the contradictory information.

"Sarah, I can almost hear you sifting through your visions. Don't you see? Your visions have always been about the past. Maybe you are seeing something that already happened. Maybe you are confused."

As much as I wanted to believe Mary, that answer was too simple.

"I can't take that chance, Mary. This is different. Yolanda saw it, too."

At the mention of her name, Yolanda jolted awake. Tears streamed down her cheeks, her lips trembled, and then she screamed. "Watch out for the post! Watch out for the falling fire."

Yolanda's cries described my exact vision. My hand trembled. I could barely hold onto the cell phone, to hear Mary.

"Sarah, are you okay? What's happening?"

"Mary, I've got to go warn Jake. See if you can get close to the fire truck so I can give Yolanda to you."

'"NO! Stay put. It's too dangerous, whatever you're thinking. Damn it, Sarah, I'm too far away to help you. I'm back at the store."

I dropped the phone as Yolanda's arms folded across her face, fending off the imagined falling post. I grabbed her hands, kissed them, and then her cheeks. Her sobs told me she was still inside her dream, which I feared was the same as my vision.

"Yoyo, honey, wake up. You're having a bad dream. Sweetie, I have you in my arms. You're okay."

With Yolanda's legs and arms wrapped around me, my walk was clumsy and heavy. She weighed more than I expected, but the solidity of her body against mine gave me strength. Her breath, her heartbeat, and the unconscious squeezes from her thighs throbbed life into me. I looked over her head, searching for Jake. He was standing by the ladder against the house, running hoses up to the attic window. I didn't dare bring Yolanda with me. I agreed with Mary, it was too dangerous and Yolanda was too much like myself, wandering with a purpose but without thinking.

Most of the crowd from the parade had dispersed. Clouds of smoke filled the sky, making the day feel like night. My feet were frozen in my indecision. I had no plan, only the knowledge that I had to prevent a tragedy. With a racing heart I turned my back to the house and started walking back toward my store. Three blocks seemed miles away.

It took me a few seconds to hear my name being called.

"Sarah, Sarah, let me help you. Sarah, Mary sent me to either stop you or help you."

There in front of me stood the Mad Hatter, Mary's cowboy husband, still dressed in his parade costume. "Rusty! Can you take Yolanda back to her mother? I have to warn Jake about a roof beam that is going to fall from the attic ceiling."

I waited for his distrust, the raised eyebrow, the snide remark.

Instead, Rusty just nodded his head and extended his arms. "I know you've got a feeling. Mary explained it all to me. I reckon it's like the feelings my grandma would get about the weather, a visiting cousin, or my uncle who died overseas. She never could explain her feelings, but we always listened to her."

Rusty's palms faced upward as if in a monastery prayer. I was beginning to wonder if Mary had made it up that he was a cowboy. He seemed more like a benevolent teacher. I tried to remember Mary's description of their relationship, but all that came to mind was their rodeo trips. She never mentioned this man's loyalty or compassion. I had a vague recollection of him tending to a horse's sore hoof throughout the night. I made a mental note to revisit Mary's sudden elopement.

Yoyo must have sensed Rusty's calmness, as she easily slipped from my arms into an embrace around neck. Half awake, she whispered, "Sarah, you have to open the closet, otherwise you won't see them."

I kissed the top of her head, patted Rusty on the shoulder, and waved them off. Jake was nowhere in sight by the time I had reversed my direction and headed toward the house. No one stopped me from crossing the yard. I feared this meant that they were too occupied with the escalating fire, until I realized that I had slipped into one of the fire jackets from Jake's truck as Yolanda and I waited out of harm's reach. Part of the weight I had attributed to Yoyo belonged to this insulated protection. Without Yoyo's body pressing into me, my arms and legs wobbled. The yellow jacket covering most of my body made me invisible to the firemen's focused efforts.

Invisible or not, I wasn't going to chance anyone stopping me from getting into the house. I circled around to the back of the house, hoping that the firemen had placed an escape ladder alongside the house. With such a small department, chances were that most of the firemen were out front or inside. Sure enough, the abandoned ladder stood ready, almost as if awaiting my arrival. I could feel the weight of the fire jacket as I mounted the ladder. Sweat formed around the crown of my head and dripped down my collar. I ignored the heat of my efforts and felt my chest tightening with the strain of the ladder's angle, the smoke, and my fear. My eyes stung from the airborne ashes, unemotional tears working to fight the irritants. I couldn't allow myself to feel now. I'd made it to the window's ledge without seeing another fireman. The last push up took all my energy. I had to hoist myself over the hooks that held the ladder to the wall and in through the window. My short legs made an awkward leap, and I felt the floor as I crumpled forward.

As I entered the room, I blinked my eyes back into focus. If I remembered the floor plan correctly, I was slightly below the attic and inside the kids' bedroom. The room was an empty shell. Blackened walls, burnt throw carpet and ashes. I could hear the firemen tromping on the stairwell and in the other rooms. Apparently they hadn't found anyone in this room. I looked up at the ceiling, expecting to see a beam burning. Nothing. The walls were flat, the ceiling arched but without any horizontal support. I doubted my vision, Yolanda's nightmare.

Frustrated, I leaned my tired body against the wall and slumped into a squat. Resting my head on my knees, I closed my eyes and tried to settle what I was seeing in front of me and what I had maybe imagined. I'd seen the hazy waving of two figures in the window. The vision of the burning beam falling still made my heart race. Yolanda, Jake, and I couldn't all be wrong.

Slowly I raised my head, this time not looking at the walls or ceiling. I focused on the floor. It was warm to the touch, but not hot. On my hands and knees I followed the heat. As I crossed from the window toward the center, I noticed a slight deviation in the floor. Soot coated the entire floor, but at this spot the black-filled grooves formed a pattern. The outline of a body, the hips and spine pressed into the floor boards. I shuddered and screamed Jake's name over and over.

Jake and about six other firemen came running. They found me on all fours, howling. I could tell from Jake's ash-stained face that he was both furious and scared to see me. His Adam's apple moved up and down as he swallowed his words.

"Damn it, Sarah, what are you doing here? I told you to stay put. Whatever it is that drew you here is important. Just tell me."

I'd known this man less than a month, and already he was anticipating my intentions.

"I saw a burning beam ready to fall. Yolanda woke from a nightmare with this same vision."

"Is that it? Is that why you're here? You could've had my men radio me this news. If you knew anything about fires, you'd know that it takes a really hot fire and a long time for a beam to burn through. Besides, this house wasn't constructed with beams. Tell me you came because of something more."

It hadn't occurred to me not to come personally with my message. My visions aren't always accurate or clear. I had to see for myself, discover the missing links in what I saw and felt.

I didn't know how to answer. Jake stared at me in anticipation of some truth. His eyes coaxed me on, his belief in my abilities felt somewhat unnerving, yet he was waiting for my lead. I started backing up, retreating towards the window. Jake took my wrist, then my hands. His blue eyes peered straight into mine.

"What else made you come?"

I saw his sisters in his eyes, his sadness, concern, and a flicker of hope. With that, words came tumbling out.

"Yolanda warned me about a closet. I think she was right and wrong at the same time. The girls must have been playing in the attic window, and then I think they disappeared somewhere below this spot. See the pattern of ashes. They collect in the grooves."

Jake bent down on his knees feeling the floor, the temperature differences. He nodded at the firemen.

"Make sure everyone is clear down below. I can see the outline of a trap door. If there was anything inside, most likely it was destroyed. Let's hope, Sarah, that this isn't what we're looking for."

"I can't go. Not until I know the girls are okay and that no one is hurt."

Jake ignored my comments. He hadn't suggested I'd leave, but two firemen were by my side, as if I were the problem. They were listening to the instructions of their captain, but had no faith in my visions or my presence.

The trap door opened with the help of a crowbar. It was if the heat had sealed it closed. I don't know what I expected Jake to find, but I found my fists tightly clenched, pressing against my mouth.

It smelled more like a campfire than a burnt home. Small puffs of smoke slowly seeped upward, and Jake disappeared from my sight. I couldn't help but call out in a hoarse, squeaky voice.

"Jake, what's down there?"

"Sarah, it's okay. There are no bodies, no children."

Relief set in for a second. I found my breath and almost relaxed, until I realized we had to keep looking. I was surer than ever that my visions were real.

It took forever for Jake to emerge from the hidden room. He came up holding a charred miniature dollhouse.

"This should have been burnt to a crisp. I can't imagine why the fire didn't destroy the dollhouse. Maybe it was coated with a special fire-retardant spray."

I nodded at Jake, but I felt a chill go up my spine. The dollhouse was a replica of the house we were in. A small wooden beam had slipped from the ceiling and lay diagonally. It was as if the beam had been pulled out, removed, not burnt as I had envisioned. I looked for it on the floor of the hidden room, but I found nothing. And then I remembered Yoyo's words, "Sarah, look in the closet. Otherwise you'll miss them."

"Jake, Yoyo mentioned a closet. It wasn't in my own vision. Is there a closet in that hidden room?"

Another fireman followed Jake up, and he carried a metal box. The shriveled remains of a peanut butter sandwich, an apple core, and two fruit juices lay inside. Jake pushed the other fireman aside and rushed back into the hidden space. I heard him knocking on walls, listening for a hollow sound, then his axe breaking through a wall. Coughing, and Jakes' booming call.

"Get me some help down here! There are two little girls. They're alive, but unconscious."

Relief overwhelmed me, not a vision of the past or the future, not sadness, not an attempt at feeling. The raw emotion of joy filled my heart as tears rolled down my cheeks. Dizzy with life, I sat down in the corner, watching the rescue. Spent, I relished this moment when my and Yoyo's visions made a difference. I closed my eyes for just a second and snowballs appeared, fields of orange paint-brush covering an old ravaged forest hillside, drawing me to rest. I must have fallen asleep. I felt two arms lifting me, the smell of sweat, the sweet essence of Jake.

"Sarah, Sarah, wake up. All is well."

As I opened my eyes, I tried to smile, but Jake's lips were on mine. Soft lips. My cheeks filled with Jake's breath. Inside the yellow fireman jacket, I felt my body twist free, lightness replacing the weight of heartbreak. Jake's embrace told me more about him than my visions could ever create. Strength, softness, and desire.

When I came up for air, Jake moved his hand over my stubbly head. Somewhere along the way I had lost my head covering. I remembered Yoyo and her sisters rubbing my head, their delight, their curiosity. I finally understood.

"Jake, I know what Yoyo meant with her warning."

Jake nodded, waiting, but I think he had already figured out Yoyo's meaning.

"She didn't want us to burn up with sadness. She wanted me to have a happy hat. She wanted you to love the life you have, understand joy with sadness."

"And the hat you made for me. Will it fit that bill?"

I took his hand in mine, feeling the curve of hard work, the tight tendons. "Oh, yes, and so much more."

"Sarah, I don't think you are rusty any more or rude."

"Good."

Jake returned to the job as I walked back to my store. I knew he would be over later, after the house and children were secure. I listened to the crowds talking about the fire, the rescue of two girls, two runaways who had been living on the streets for weeks.

As I walked into my store, there stood Mary with her cowboy Mad Hatter, Yoyo, her two sisters and mother. Mary lifted me up in a bear hug, her newly-mascaraed eyes blackened with tears.

I said the first thing that came to me. "Looks like you could use a makeover."

She responded in kind. "Looks like you are ready for the future."

Knock Knock

Truth is hard to explain in a world based on logic. Through the eyes of a man growing senile, where memories and senses collide, how do you decide what is real, what is important? And will anyone listen?

The prognosis given by the doctors made no sense. Mort, her husband of almost 50 years, seemed lost, depressed, not himself. Medications deepened the problem. Selma guarded the man she loved with the vigilance of a warrior.

I know that I live in this house, but everything is so strange—out of order. I can't straighten things up, fix what is broken.

My legs are like twigs, knobby and stiff. I lift my feet, but the floor stays stuck. My head goes first, and the rest of my body reluctantly follows. Wherever I am going, the path is circular, but with sharp edges, angles that jut out. And my mind, if it was in the head that led, where did it go?

Selma called for an ambulance, not knowing what else to do. For the third time that week, Mort had fallen. The ambulance took him for an MRI to test his brain. Selma feared what they would find, feared the claustrophobic tunnel that confined them both. She paced the hospital hallways as he disappeared.

I'll tell you a story, but I don't want you to repeat this, not to anyone. It is about my sins. They'll discover them anyway, when they take the pictures. Pictures are just memories, and my memories are etched into the brain. They are all that I have.

Something is wrong in my house, and I am to blame. Why can't I stay with the good memories? The bad ones form deep grooves, but the good ones are so fleeting, they disappear just as I grab for them. It is these scars covered over by years that will give me away. The doctors look for the medical reason. Their fancy machine is a chamber of hell for me. Encased inside the tunnel, the scars give out torturous echoes of my past indiscretions. I'm deafened by the echoes. They pierce my heart.

I wear no badges of honor, nothing metallic to set off alarms. My service to my country was bound to home ports. As a Navy Pharmacist Mate I almost followed in the footsteps of my dad. But my dance was different. Hair slicked back, white bellbottoms stiff with purpose, I learned the art of stitching and mending. But I also learned that appearances keep words coming, that as I helped and administered, I gained confidences. Over poker, the men in my unit shared their dreams, their drugs, their women. By day I gave first aid, by night I touched bareness. Passion ignited by drugs, by fear, by greed, so explosive that it left me like a desert. I found solace in folding my clothes, sorted in neat piles by color and use. I cut my nails and cuticles, leaving just a thin line of white encircling the edge of my fingertips. Clear polish, transparent and clean enough for surgery, hardened nails for a gentleman.

I tap my nails urgently against the chamber, wanting out of this cell. "Knock knock, is anybody there?" I tap but no one comes. I have to behave like that gentle soul they know and love, yet I remain a shell, for I have sold that soul many times over.

Selma paced outside, smoking her third cigarette. A nurse found her and reported that he was agitated, emotional.

Time keeps traveling even though I can't move. I'm caught now with a child eating peanuts at the zoo. She is holding my hand, palm to palm, sticky fingers entwined in mine. Hers are sticky with cotton candy. I need a handkerchief to wipe her fingers off, but she only smiles with big brown

*eyes. I try not to cry. I leave tomorrow for New York—gone
again for weeks. My suitcase packed with tailored suits. I
prepare for my sales pitch, pitching the likelihood of richness,
the American Dream. My bedroom eyes hypnotize the
women into giving up their savings, and the men see green:
part envy, part scam. Yet my eyes are really grey. I am a
chameleon. Who am I?*

*I almost doze, but the echoes of my memories wake
me, bouncing my lids open. I can't close them now to return
to sleep. I always napped on my trips. The guys would make
fun of me. The late nights, after the pitching, take a toll.
I curl up and rest my brain, my body. I'd rather believe in
the sticky fingers of cotton candy than the stickiness of the
late night wanderings. I never want to travel again. Strange
hotel rooms, one night stands. The echoes frighten me into
wakefulness. Hours drag into years. And the worry chops
me up.*

As the nurse wheeled Mort back to his room,
Selma rushed over to him. She stared at his face, noticed
the tears, the sad worry.

*I feel the warmth of long, soft fingers pressed gently
into my face. These fingers belong to my wife—the bride with
long legs, a winning smile, and an open heart. I return to her
after weeks on the road. I am the King of the household. My
stories fill the air. Gathered at the dinner table, my family
listens to all my jokes. I am the funny man. I pitch them
my days, never my nights. My food misses my mouth, my
hands shake and I stumble with words. How many bites can
I swallow? How much truth do I even remember?*

Selma let the nurse's aide dress Mort. He was
slow to rise, staring at the floor, at the door and the
windows. Selma supervised, wishing for her fastidious,
handsome husband to emerge. She turned Mort to face
the mirror, smiling with all the love of their history.

The floor is cold, hard against my bare feet. I look

at my toes that need a manicure. The nail on my big toe is mustard-colored and thick. I'm offended that it even exists. My beard and hair are now the same length. If I look in the mirror I see a stranger in the house. Why did my wife let him in? He isn't even dressed and it is the middle of the day. What was she thinking, disregarding safety, compromising our privacy; unless she is having an affair. I watch as she approaches and places her warm hands on his shoulders. She turns him gently, guiding him to a chair. She bends down and kisses the top of his head. No mouth kisses, no touching of lips to lips. If she had, I'd know our marriage was over.

Selma smoked one more cigarette, two puffs, as the aide helped Mort into the car. She worried about stopping, worried about the wheelchair, worried that Mort would worry about her and not listen to reason. What was in his head?

It is hot outside, unbearably so. The temperature has risen to 115 degrees and the air chokes to breathe. The lady at my side insists I get out. She is persuasive, telling me she has to buy a carafe for the coffee machine. She won't leave me alone, so I go. I have to protect her. She is so fragile. I let her drive the Lexus but make sure the gas tank is filled. You can't forget to fill the tank up. On my many road trips I always had maps detailing every gas station and rest stop. I knew in advance if the weather was going to turn. My rule was never to let the tank go below the half mark. If a storm came up or if you got lost, you'd at least have enough gas to get you to somewhere safe. I am lost now. The roads to the store are unfamiliar. I have so little energy left to even look out the window. What is the point in fueling myself? I have nowhere to go.

Stacks of photo albums line the table tops. Even the walls contain frames of my life. I am surrounded by smiling faces, girls morphing to women. These ladies belong to me. I know this because they have their arms around me, heads tilted toward me. I see them grow and multiply. I am a father, grandfather. Cheek to cheek, eyelash kisses and hugs. I sit behind a mahogany desk that shines my image back. Across from me sits the prosecutor, the spiritual muse, and a gallery of jurors who have come to judge my deeds.

They grew up and left me with my sins. The desk is too big, my head too small to hold on to my defense. I am sure we will be evicted from the house when they find out.

Selma ate only a sandwich, Mort a glass of Ensure. She yearned for a glass of wine, but didn't dare. Her new bed, the den couch, welcomed her. As the long day finally ended, Selma fell asleep.

There is someone tapping on the outside window that leads to the golf course. Maybe it is a dream: the tapping of shoes in a ballroom, the tapping of impatience. The noise is too loud. Why isn't anyone else up in this place? I pull the blinds back slowly. This has to be a dream. A small frightened angel bangs on my porch door at 3:00 a.m. I scream. I don't even believe what my eyes see. I don't trust anyone, not even myself. Fear attaches me to the door until the screams bring the lady of the night. I warn her not to open the door. Be careful. It is real. There is a lost child sitting in my living room. The police are everywhere. I sit bewildered, stare out into the black night while the little girl eats cookies and milk. She acts as if this is normal, that good people will always open doors for her. I sit staring out into that blackness knowing she is wrong.

The police finally left after what seemed an eternity. Selma, drained from the emotion, looked over Mort, the hero in a bizarre story. He didn't understand the confusion, the significance of his instinct. Selma doubted her own sanity more than Mort's. She had dozed while a little girl wandered the golf course, searching for her parents. Negligent parents to have left a child asleep in the car, or was this an accident, or worse yet, a bright child seeking help? Selma cleaned up the cookies, wondering if her Mort might slip away, too. Would he wake alone as a man or as a four-year-old child?

Day comes too soon and not soon enough. I sleep more than my allotted share, but I never feel rested. Why is it that day is no different than night? I wonder where I can hide so the bogey men won't get me. When my little girl had nightmares about fires, I told her to think of rain and all the bright colors of the rainbow. The rain would stifle the fire and the rainbow would guide her out of the darkness. I sit inside this body that can't run, can't play the game—tennis or golf or any semblance of propriety. The sun shines so brightly that I have to wear sunglasses, darkening the light. The bogey men are long gone, yet they sit inside my scarred brain.

How do I get them to leave? I don't want any bad memories. I don't want to sit here worrying about the lady of my life. Why does she stay with me?

I hear her talking on the phone, whispering. "Shh, he might hear me. I don't what him to know…" She hides so much from me, like I'm a child. If it were only so easy, I could sit in the corner facing the wall. After my time out, my sentence would be over. I'd be free to forget stealing time, love, and money. Her devotion to me must be evidence of something good.

Selma left the front door opened just a crack so she could watch Mort. Hopefully he'd sleep while she called her children. She carved a slice of fresh air to pollute ten times a day with her nasty cigarette habit. Her wall-less room, the stucco patio entranceway that separated each condo from the next, calmed her. Here she would think, work the hardest of hard Sudoku puzzles, and smoke. Smoking was her meditation, her exercise, her salvation. This was where she lied to her children, sharing only the small truths of her feelings.

"Ma, I can't hear what you are saying. Why are you whispering? Is Dad okay?"

"Don't worry, everything is *fine*. Your father is a hero. He saved a four-year-old last night."

Selma used her code word *fine*. Her children tried to decipher when to come to her rescue. They wondered what was real.

Have I told you the story about when I sold carpets with my brother? He'd install them and I'd close the deal. We lost lots of money in that venture. I can't use a hammer or fix plumbing. I sold, he fixed. Neither of us were collectors. I sit here collecting dust. I am like the creaky floors. Carpet can only hide, not change what is inside.

Country Villa

*So many of us are sandwiched between the needs of aging
parents, adult children, and our own health issues. This
story explores dedication, love, and patience—a reminder to
count blessings.*

I walk the nursing home halls lined with
medicine and food carts, populated with men and
women dressed in royal blue, white on white or some
cheery pastel print. They are the attendants who take
care of the people who live here. They are all people
with stories, I'm sure, but some have left them so far
behind that they are no longer present in the past, and
know no future.

My father is here and he is a lucky man—lucky
because he has potential, lucky because his wife, my
mother, is vigilant. She passes nine hours a day here. It
is her job. Ever so elegant, she twists her long grey locks
into a bun, dons her signature wool pants, turtleneck
top, and white dangling earrings. The cigarettes are
never far from her reach. She is dressed to make an
impression. She has to impress upon herself and her
husband the importance of caring, of attending to life.
She coos him to attention.

She worries about insurance, falling stock
markets, dwindling funds, and the logistics of living,
while my dad just wants to know the name of where
he is.

Today I have to return home, thousands of miles
north of this desert. I enter his room, pushing open
the closed door. This door is the only separation he has
from the group. My mother insisted on a private room,
a place where he can hide from so many unwanted

realities. He rustles in his bed, looking up, startled at my entrance.

"I must have dozed. Have you been here long?"

I don't have a chance to answer as Jose, the daytime nurse's aide, wheels in his breakfast. Two aides lift the white sheet under his body and hoist his body up so that his head reaches the top of the bed, and then they hit the left green button to raise him to sitting. There is no time to brush his teeth, no time to attend to the transition of one day into the next. Food arrives abruptly.

"Dad, I just got here. You must have slept well last night."

"Tell me, is this the Country Club?"

I know he isn't making a joke, but it feels like it. He can't hold onto the name of where is. He only can read signs, and the road to this place is Country Club.

"Close, Dad. You are at the rehab center, Country Villa."

"Can I ask you something, Abbe?"

Just by the ominous sound of his voice, I know he is searching, wanting answers. I don't want my father to look to me for answers. I want to revert back to when he knew everything. I want to go back to when I called him Poppy, the man in my life who would pop up at all crucial times to save me.

"Anything, Poppy."

"What do I do if I have to go BM?"

I look into his green eyes, and all I see is worry and wonder. It is a question of a toddler trying to work out the logistics of how everything in his body works.

"Poppy, they can help you. Do you remember when they helped you a couple of days ago? You press the red button and the nurse's aide helps you get onto the raised seat in the bathroom."

"Do they watch me, or can I have my privacy?"

He says this with an edge to his voice, almost a demand. He is at the mercy of others for his dignity. Dignity is more important than the French toast, or the oatmeal that slides down his parched throat. He couldn't care less if there is a melon he can taste or if the sausage looks like a turd. That pales next to the question of why his legs don't work or why he folds in half and his trunk weighs a ton. He trusts that my mother or my sister or I will make sure he gets around. His worry is the release of crap.

"Once you are seated, they can close the door. There is a long cord to pull that triggers a red light outside of the bathroom when you've finished your business."

"Oh, I just wanted to know because I have business to do."

And this is when it hits me. My father's business is what we take for granted. His business of living is reduced to something less than the basics. His world now revolves around the logistics of decisions so easy for me to make that I don't even bat an eyelash.

Jose comes in to help my father after he pushes away the breakfast. Jose smiles and says, "*No problema.*" His answer to this request is simple. He doesn't see it as a problem because he can help. He is trained to help everyone here to feel like this isn't a big deal.

I wait outside in front of the Country Villa, walking the grounds. Today is a weekend, and not many of the residents are up. One lady is already dressed and in her wheelchair knitting bright patches for what I imagine is a quilt for her large extended family. They were all here yesterday, sitting on the benches, lined up in front of her. She recognizes me and smiles. I greet her in Spanish. I don't want to speak in English, preferring to recognize her reality, denying my own. We continue talking about her family's visit, the vibrant colors of her wool, until I walk past waving. Abruptly my fears creep back and I'm thinking in my own language wondering what will be. "*Que sera, sera,*" whatever will be, will be. These are the words of my childhood song: "Will I be pretty, will I be happy? Whatever will be, will be, *que sera, sera.*"

A handsome man, deeply tanned, with a full head of white hair and a blue shirt, sits in his wheelchair enjoying the first rays of sun and what I presume is his first cigarette of the day. *The Wall Street Journal* is in his lap, which is bordered by his left leg amputated at the knee, and the right leg, adorned with a white bandage. He is waiting for someone to pick him up for an outing. I imagine that my mother will start talking with him when she takes her needed smoke breaks. He is fully present, knowing his past and clearly what his future brings. His strong arms push his wheelchair more into the sun. He takes charge. I am sure that his bulging biceps can lift his trunk off and onto the bathroom chair, and that his business would have nothing to do with defecation. He appears to be a movie star waiting for his lover.

My father, my dad, my Poppy, is now ready for the challenges of the day. He sits up straight where they have placed him. Brenda, the occupational therapist, tells me that he has dressed himself.

"Dad, that's great. I didn't know you could do all of that."

"I didn't know I could, either."

I can feel the irony hanging in the air. My mother, my sister, and I are incredulous. There is so much to explore in that statement. What exactly can my father do? I refuse to go backward. Life isn't made that way.

To explore the past somehow takes me away from the present. I'd have to measure the losses, the reasons that led us to believe that my father was more helpless, and maybe place blame. None of this matters.

Brenda works my father hard. You can see it in his eyes, the set of his jaw and the shaking right knee. His body slides to the right due to the most recent stroke. It is as if he is an overstuffed doll, a dummy placed in the chair that without support slides off. Brenda commands, "Push down on your left, Mort, lift yourself up."

I place my hand gently on my father's left buttock. I whisper, "Dad, make your left butt cheek meet my hand. Now raise your head and chest."

He is straight, sitting in awe. The world has become upright, and he pays attention. Each time he starts to slip, I touch his left side. Eventually he catches himself.

All day long he practices sitting up straight. Just as Brenda casually stated that my father dressed himself, I can say, "Dad you sat up straight today."

There are tears in his eyes. I know he is going to cry, that it is so hard to be brave. He tries to hide the tears, but they are too big, his cheeks aren't catching them, and his shirt is getting wet. Silently I hand him a tissue.

When he has gained his composure, he looks at me in wonder. "There is too much to do. I'll never be able to stand or walk on my own."

I'm standing in front of my father in his wheelchair. I take his hands and look him the eye. "Do you know all that you did today? You sat up on your own, helped with your shower, dressed yourself, walked with Brenda's help, and learned how to sit up straight. You did so much."

"But there is too much left to learn."

"Dad, you did way more than we thought you could. Let's just measure what you have accomplished, not what you haven't."

He is staring at me, head held up high, both shoulders even with the top of the wheelchair. His eyes are fixed on mine.

"You're not bullshitting me, are you?"

"I'd never bullshit you, Dad."

He nods, accepting my words as if they mattered more than anything. I take his hands and see that they are flaking. His paper-thin skin is so dry, needs so much moisture. As I rub hand cream into them, gradually it seeps into the pores, and they become alive. I unfurl each finger, lengthen them and move my hands through his—all of his life passes through his fingers to mine. I feel him so vibrantly, so intimately.

I go home today, and my father remains in the Country Villa. He is so lucky to have my mother watching over him. Devoted, she adds energy to a place filled with losses.

They say that energy begets energy. I can tell that those patients who have visitors look you in the eye, smile. Those who have been left slump over, look away to a distant place of memories.

I wonder if their hands are dry, if the love held within can be released. I must remember to offer my hands as well my embraces to all those I love.

A-Musings

You've Got a Match

The language of relationships throughout history takes on modern-day internet dating services as compared to times of match-making. Matters of the heart are timeless.

I can hear my mother's voice as if it were just yesterday. "Just add a little blush to your cheeks. You need color. Mascara will highlight your big eyes. You've got really nice eyes."

The only problem is that the voice I now hear is that of my youngest daughter. She lives with me and is witnessing my re-entry into the world of dating.

I really haven't dated yet, but I could, maybe. As a teenager I was everyone's best friend, the ones boys confided in but never asked out. I was alternately the object of their wet dreams with the accompanying snide remarks concerning my voluptuous breasts, or I was in high demand as a study partner. Good grades were essential for the football team. Now I am the woman that businessmen find stimulating to talk with, flirt with, share confidences, and ask advice on negotiations.

Discovering that at fifty-four I look more beautiful, more real and appealing to the opposite sex, hasn't changed how I feel on the inside. I don't truly understand the rules of the dating game.

On a plane ride from Salt Lake City to my home town of Bellingham, WA, a man seated in my row said as I approached, "Thank goodness you are small." He stood up, bumping his head as he let me in.

Instead of just nodding and letting his comment go, I said what I thought. "So how big was the other passenger?"

"He weighed over 300 pounds and spilled over into my seat. It was a three-hour torturous flight."

I could have offered my sympathies and passed pleasantries. What came out was a challenge. "Too bad for him. You only had to endure three hours of discomfort. He has to live with discomfort for his entire life."

Oddly enough, this man asked me out on a date three months later. An industrial psychologist, he challenged and analyzed every statement I made, drank two scotches within twenty minutes, and insisted that we go Dutch. I wrote him off as a man with issues.

So far I have been propositioned by two business associates, one actually aggressively pursuing my favors in bed, the other just leaving hints. I met a true soul-mate along the way, wrote copious e-mails, waited by the phone for calls, even felt the twitter of butterflies at the sound of his voice. I hurt so deeply when after a year of business and friendship, he disappeared. I lost sleep, became edgy and irritable, until I understood that I was supposed to feel good, not bad, in a relationship. I've converted my love for him into the love I would have for a brother. This allows me to care but not get caught in a stream of anticipation.

Repeating my teen years is agony. Then I could blame my awkwardness on an abundance of hormones and the tantalizing promise of my voluptuous breasts. Now my hormones are arrested, yet more potent when aroused. My breasts droop slightly, fall more gracefully when cleverly supported, and promise friendship and comfort. At least then I knew who was in my league. Now I have no judge of ages. I'm physically attracted to men 10 to 15 years my junior, and men 10 to 15 years my senior come a-calling.

I've kept myself open to all relationships. Gaining

from the wisdom of a man turned 80 and dying, I passed twenty-four Thursday afternoons talking. He would come in his convertible Miata to court me with stories, talk politics, and share his view on the day. His last six months showed me depth, kindness, and vitality for living. He taught me to redefine love and not to mourn what is gone, but to celebrate what one has. He gave me and all his friends the gift of acknowledgement.

I get confused between eras—hearing my mother's voice, that of my daughter, and whispers from the spirit of my grandmother. "Be ready, you never know what is around the corner."

Upon the urging of friends and my sister, I entered the new age of match-making. Match-making for my grandmother, who came from Russia, involved a family promise, no chance of sensing love before finding oneself married. Hers was a marriage of convenience and financial necessity, just like the story of *Fiddler on the Roof*. My grandmother made a choice, which I believe was to create magic no matter what the circumstances. She raised three sons and a daughter, my mom, while she ran a neighborhood grocery store. There are no stories about my grandfather, my namesake. I can only hope that the match worked and that the lessons of hope, optimism, and love were passed down the generations to me.

My match-making service comes by e-mail. What is the most important thing in your life? What sports do you enjoy? How would you like to spend your Saturday evenings? Where do you see yourself in 15 years? I answer these questions as if this were the exam of my life. I'm being judged on my answers. Should I let them know that I am addicted to coffee candies, that when I write I forget about everyone, and that I have a hard time not being passionate? I attach a photo of me looking athletic and one with a black dress that reveals both my cleavage and my legs. At first I act like a kid when my e-mail pops up with, "You've got a Match." It is almost an addiction reading the descriptions, checking pictures. And then it isn't.

I'm not exactly old-fashioned, more retro like the PT Cruiser I drive. I want to meet someone in the flesh, get a sense of their style by the flash of a smile, the tilt of a head, the excitement of a voice. I want romance that includes acknowledgement equal to that of my 80 year-old friend. I want the soulful insights and humorous jokes of my friend turned brother. I want all the married men who find my conversations interesting to make sure they dance with their wives. I've purchased mascara and a little blush because you never know who you'll meet just around the corner.

Horsetail

*As in many of the tales I spin, this one takes a new
perspective, that of the weed with its enduring power,
beauty, and simplicity.*

Light, airy lime-green stems with feather swirls
appear after a good rain. They seem to have risen out
of nowhere to overtake the garden bed. To me they are
a carpet of beauty that must be plucked. Young and
vulnerable, they can be pulled out easily. Later, as they
grow, the feather swirls disappear and the asparagus
stems grow tall and thick with black rings. The swirls
before they bolt become stiff scrub brushes.

My love affair with the horsetail is harmless
but complicated. The plants endure because they root
themselves so solidly in the ground. Their rhizome-
like roots travel fast and furiously, growing stronger
if you miss them as you pull. Their stem cap is filled
with spores that burst and take flight to spread with
the wind.

I know they can become invasive, ousting our
cultured flowering friends. But horsetails are rushes—
coming in quick, declaring their space. I love their
simplicity. They make me feel free, unencumbered and
sexy. The twirl of leaves, swishing with the breeze,
the varied hues of greens as they progress in stages
of growth, the cone caps that soar upward, reaching,
searching, are mine in a simple glance.

Tall grasses, tight-knit sedum, and the velvet leaf
of lamb's ear seduce me into the garden. The Gunnera
with its elephant leaves embraces me. I love the wisp
of the red Japanese maple, and I'm partial to the perfect
white flower of the trillium and the cotton tufts of goat's

beard. But it is the insidious horsetail that captures my fancy. I pluck it with love, knowing no matter what I do, it will return. I welcome it with an open heart.

Foundations

Fundamental principles of mechanics, philosophy, and society merge to make crazy sense out of life.

Since before I knew the questions to ask, or the concepts of construction, government, or business, my curiosity sought to understand the insides. My Bubbie use to say to me, "It is what is on the inside that counts." I interpreted this to mean either that the outside didn't count, or that the inside held all the mystery. Later I'd learn about the concepts of superficial beauty, but my deep connection to infrastructure began with not understanding the nuances of adult speak.

A few years ago I attended the Citizens Police Academy Class, six weeks of learning the art of policing. On the police website there is a picture of me dressed in bomb gear—gear that weighs three times my own weight and flatters the Pillsbury Doughboy with a look of macho-metal. I volunteered to feel and understand the heat, the claustrophobic sense of maneuvering under stress. I became the comic relief, the Police Doughgirl, waddling along the halls, attempting the impossible, swallowed within a purpose.

Carpenters create from the inside out. The large building constructed in front of my restaurant, which blocked my view and hindered entrance to the parking lot, became my nine-month fascination with the diggers, the pillars of rebar, framing, plumbing, wiring, lifting of walls. The bridge overhead connected my business to the new edifice that now houses the bank where I deposit my meager earnings. I marvel at how easy it is to see only the end result and to forget the innards of the world.

Growing up, I often wondered about size. I believed that my short stature came from my Bubbie, and that my chest also skipped a generation, endowing me with breasts twice my frame size and overwhelmingly larger than my mother's. Looking at my small infrastructure, I knew that a problem brewed. How to run and play? What to do with the flopping? I needed a flopper-stopper, an over-the-shoulder-boulder-holder. There was a name for this—a bra.

Bra engineers liken the design of a bra to building a bridge. The challenge of vertical forces of gravity blended with the horizontal earth movement of wind resembles the forces women experience running or turning their body. Not only must a system be designed to enclose and support a semi-solid mass of variable volume and shape, but its adjacent mirror image. Two breasts must function as one.

The vast possibilities of designs multiplied once bra engineers realized the complexities of asymmetrical shapes, that each breast had its own form, and that distributing the weight evenly over the torso not only had to work in the front but in the back as well. Here is a trick my Bubbie taught me. If the band that encircles the body rides up the woman's back, the bra is too loose. If the band digs into the back, the bra is too tight. Since women can't see backwards, they can test this by reversing the bra on the torso, so that the cups are in the back. Trust me—if engineers built bridges this way, we would have pointed armor that arched toward water.

The wear and tear on our vast system of bridges eventually gives in to gravity. Sagging follows. The inevitable but fixable problem historically is one of infrastructure. Designers created the wonder bra that pushes up, or the jogging bra that flattens down. And it is here that I venture to declare my age, and evoke the adult speak of my Bubbie. We must be concerned with inner beauty, not the superficial aesthetics of fleeting beauty.

While the government wisely uses our taxes to repair roads and bridges, I alone can shore up my droppers. On a mission, I ventured into the lingerie department at Macy's Department Store. Greeted by thousands of hanging breast bands, I panicked. The history of the feminine mystique lay before me. I was not here to flaunt my cleavage, nor to add volume with padding or jiggle gels. Echoing the voices of my youth and my aged body, I still wanted function instead of fashion. To my delight, I found comfort. Among the offerings I found a cross between a jogging bra and soft formed cup with back clips. It didn't matter if I was short or tall, lopsided or voluptuous. The material held a memory—soft and forgiving.

With my foundation secure, I now move with a sense of beauty and ease. No one can see what lies beneath the sweater, only I know. My advice remains simple: confidence starts with a good foundation.

TOE

From an early age, I longed to be both a comedian and a spy. The acute awareness and intelligence of both professions have been my guiding lights. I write instead.

Simplicity should never be underestimated. Distill whatever your thoughts are to the basic. If that doesn't work, start over. The most simplistic thought involves the complexity of the universe: We are one.

I have five toes on each foot.

I made this discovery when I was in the crib. I can almost remember the first time I stuck my big toe in my mouth. Some kids sucked their thumbs, but I was already the show-off bending and twisting my body in contortions.

My five toes bind me to humanity. We of the human race are pentadactyl, as are most of the ancestors we descended from. With great pride we differentiate ourselves because we can stand upright and walk. Four-footed mammals also have five toes, but they are considered digitigrades. Instead of walking with the soles of their feet on the ground, they walk on their toes. Digitigrades are quiet and fast.

I can remember the times when I walked tippy-toed through the house, sneaking downstairs to listen to my parents' hushed voices. I'd scamper up before they found I had been eavesdropping. I'd be the antelope, gracefully exiting—fast, sure, silent-footed. Only my panting and giggles gave me away. Once discovered, I planted my toes firmly on the steps and "solefully" ran to my room. My prize was the laughter from the adults. Humor makes the world go round.

My father's name is Morton. I discovered he was

142 • Tattle Tales

famous one day when we were shopping at the grocery store. Morton's Salt and Morton's Pie were both named in his honor. Unbeknownst to me, he has a toe named after him as well. Morton's toe is the second toe, right next to the big, rounded first toe. It isn't a Morton's toe unless it reaches beyond the hallux, another name for the big fat toe, and is accompanied by a hyper mobile metatarsal segment and an accompanying callus, loose and rough.

Only about 10% of the people worldwide have this special toe, which, depending on the culture, can be a good or bad thing. Some see it as the grasping toe, ever so useful for picking up items. Others believe it to be a sign of intelligence or a sign of beauty. Since the invention of shoes, however, Morton's toe represents only pain.

Shoes started the conspiracy to sexualize women's feet. High heels, straps wrapping up along the calves, and pointed tips are amongst the great efforts the industry has gone to transform our utilitarian feet into something out of a myth. With my 4'11" stature, high heels could be part of my wardrobe, a prop to level the playing ground. However, the 4" heels only serve to make me walk like a drunk, wincing with cramped calves and a stifled mind.

Toes now have another purpose. They no longer are meant to be functional. Toe cleavage is the answer to a question that I can't even formulate. The Classic Pump specializes in selling shoes with low-cut vamps. Low-cut shoes reveal toe cleavage, just as a low-cut top reveals breast cleavage. The art of sexy shoes is to show only the first two cracks.

Toes are simple appendages, *dedos de pie*, fingers of the feet. They are meant to be free, unencumbered.

I have five toes on each foot.
They are virgins, unpainted.
Sandals show off all of my toes and the spaces in between.
I go barefoot whenever I can.

The **Theory of Everything** lets us run wild with imagination, allows us to touch this earth with our feet, fly in our minds to the unthinkable. This is where everything counts, has a purpose, whether understood or not.

Time **O**ver **E**ffort
Tame **O**r **E**ffervescent
Tantalizing **O**vert **E**mulating
This **O**ur **E**ternity

You can't pick your toes, but you can pick your friends.
Pick wisely.

Travels

Sri Lanka

My goal as a traveler is to visit places that remove me from my comfort zone. A small dot of a country that rests near India, Sri Lanka seemed more accessible in size and people. Here I learned of lost civilizations, religion, political strife, rituals, and the beauty of the land.

Sri Lanka sits atop the Indian Ocean, an ocean that I never dreamed I'd see. Maps are flat, and even the globe can't bring the history and the fauna and people to life. To fully understand Sri Lanka, I sweat in the heat of the tropics, feel the passion that the equatorial latitude brings with its currents from Europe, China, and Indonesia, and along the Marco Polo trade routes from the Portuguese, Dutch, and British. What stays with me is the singular focus on living within a divided culture.

Like love, I do not separate out the parts of Sri Lankan people I like. I accept what I see. They are as complex as they are simple. Uniforms tell me what an individual does, blue for the navy, brown for the police, and green for the army. The military is ever-present, accepted and still needed to maintain a tenuous peace between the Sinhalese and Tamils. The city sweepers wear orange t-shirts, the hotel servers don matching sarongs, and the Hindu women distinguish themselves, not only by the sari they wear, but with an oval red dot between their brows. Muslim men wear caps, their women covered all in black with eyes peeking out from slotted scarves. The Buddhist monks are wrapped in bright orange, the women are covered, and the men work clad in sarongs. The Christians wear clothes that are less noticeable, yet this too distinguishes them with just a glance. None of these clues reveal who these individuals are.

Religion divides as well as unites. A caste system remains even as the new wave of young folk claim they are not bound by rules of the past. Everyone knows from where they came: ruler, religious leader, cultivator, or laborer. Marrying within or above one's caste is accepted, but marrying below it takes convincing the elders to move away from old ideas. Just as the clothes tell a story, the past makes its claim.

Within these layers I sense the inborn dignity of a people who believe in the whole, despite the turmoil of a conquered past, recent terrorism from the Tamil Tigers, and the devastating effects of the 2004 tsunami. I witness the efforts of individuals coming together to achieve great feats. Reconstructing the walls of Ritigala Kingdom, a group of six men wrap rope around a stone weighing hundreds of pounds. Lifting with combined forces, they rebuild the old for the new to see. Fishermen gather in the early morning. Some push the wooden boat out, and eight men jump aboard. Once out in the open water, one lone man swims to shore holding the coconut rope attached to the net. The crew paddles, spreading the seine net across the shallows. Then with a synchronized dance, locals run along the beach forming a line, pulling the net in as the original fisherman coils the rope. The bounty of fish remains netted until the boat is dragged back on shore, making skid marks in the sand. The fisherman divvies up the tuna, sardines, bottom fish, and flounder, leaving an empty seine on the beach and arms filled with meals to come.

A family labors together soaking, shucking, beating coconut hairs, braiding rope to earn money so they can send their son to college. One old man has for the last 24 years salvaged turtle eggs from the poachers and created a turtle farm where the blind or maimed turtles live out their lives. The female turtles feed for five years and then return to the ocean. Tea pickers, covered in bright clothes, and carrying umbrellas, stand on the terraced upper hills. Bright spots of color, they toil barefooted. They wait in line to have their satchels of tea leaves weighed and taken to the tea factories. Rice paddies appear as squares quilted with dirt, flooded by the surrounding rivers through the irrigation channels. Rhythmic waves of sun-kissed hands dig deep holes to keep the water flowing. These people work together, bound by their isolation.

Infrastructure emerges differently in Sri Lanka. While I take care of bodily functions in private, the Sri Lankans pride themselves in a sense of cleanliness. They take advantage of what is, not what isn't. Men bathe in streams in the early morning. I've witnessed the daily ritual of brushing teeth by the river bed and the flock of women and children who appear after a downpour to find the irrigation channels filled with water. Dirty clothes pounded clean, children laugh as they are soaped.

Highways exist as a future wish while roads wash away. Without lines, without pavement, the chaos of cars, pedestrians, cows, and weaving drivers works. Accidents are rare. I, who hate to drive, close my eyes, hold my breath, and squeeze my stomach in as if to take up less room. Anger rarely flares. Along every route, bell-shaped stupas with Buddha shrines await offerings. Drivers face their fears with a spiritual pause to their gods. Call it faith or superstition, these offerings create a sense of well-being.

I confess that on my last day, I gave in and took a ride in a tuk-tuk. I had scorned the three-wheeled cars and the nagging drivers who wanted to take advantage of a tourist. Yet after walking for hours in the Pettah, a city of dilapidated stalls filled with every item in existence and swarming crowds, and then into the finer stores of the Cinnamon district, my legs and energy gave way. Thankfully Jim and I sat inside the enlarged scooter, while the driver wiggled between buses, delivering us safely to our hotel.

During our stay in Sri Lanka, Jagath, our driver, insulated us from the harsher aspects of Sri Lanka, but this country's unique appeal includes the less than perfect life. Jagath always met us halfway down the beach, he walking from his bungalow, we from our select boutique hotel. Each of us maintained our place in the world and on this trip. Friendships come in unexpected forms. Each of us shared what we could. It is what lies between the forms, the castes, that interests me, pulls at my heart.

Well-being comes to me in the form of exploration: the Pacific Ocean, the Atlantic and the Caribbean Oceans, and now the Indian Ocean. Inside of me is a love of people, the desire to share, and the quest for adventure. The texture of Sri Lanka—rich with the greens of tea country, the wildness of elephants, leopards, reptiles, jungle, the warmth of sun, sand, fishing, the guns of military watching even from the ramparts of Galle Fort, the 100-year-old trains passing through a hilly paradise of hard-working people, tea and spices, monkeys and cows on the streets I walk— all this fills my heart.

Love accepts. The Sri Lankans accept, see what is, dream, and improve. The Muslim morning call to prayer coexists with the downloaded cell phone ring of Lionel Richie's song, "Hello, is it me you are looking for?" I have traveled halfway around the world to accept Sri Lankan complexity and simplicity. I know exactly who I am.

In the words of the Sinhalese," *Ayubowan*, hello, *Hari hari*, okay okay…"

Carate

This trip challenged my sense of adventure on an escapade pitting nature versus man, with a humble outcome.

Costa Rica is a country of many textures, diverse in its people, land, vegetation, and wildlife. After ten days in the central mountains, where our elevation peaked at 10,000 feet above sea level, Jim and I turned our rented vehicle south and west to the Osa Penisula. We hated to leave the place where the Resplendent Quetzals made their home, and the cloud forest misted our faces and chilled our bones, but more adventures pulled us along on our journey.

Here the landscape morphed from primary oak forests to hillsides of greenery where cattle grazed and *fincas* of coffee, pineapple, and palm oil produced cash crops. These were lands modified over centuries by the toil of farmers. As we wound our way down, the sun warmed the air, so that our sweat and the smells of the salty gulf air replaced the cooler, dense air. We gradually stripped to shorts and sleeveless tops. By the time we arrived in the small town of Puerto Jimenez, our eyes scanned the skies for scarlet macaws.

Fringed on one side by the water of the Gulfo Dulce and divided in its center by a mangrove swamp, Puerto Jimenez became our transition. We walked lazily through the streets, finding the *pulperia* to stock up on wine and essentials. On a side street by the airport, we found a delightful shop with local handmade crafts and a hole in the wall restaurant where we enjoyed our morning breakfast of homemade tortillas and *huevos rancheros*. With full bellies, we headed out to Carate, the stepping-off point on the edge of Parque Nacional

Corcovado, and where our lodge awaited.

No amount of research or rest could have prepared us for what came next. The guidebooks wrote about options for traveling to Corcovado. Tourists could choose from direct flights straight into the Sirena Ranger Station, ferry rides to cross over the Gulfo Dulce, or the use of local taxis and buses to drive all the way to Carate. In small print, they all briefly mentioned that only seasoned hikers and drivers should attempt the routes from one ranger station to the next. None of the books described the insane roads into Carate.

On our way out of Puerto Jimenez, we made one last stop at the office headquarters of La Leona Eco Lodge to check our reservations. We had booked four nights at a jungle lodge far off the beaten path. The maps were unclear, showing dotted lines that seemed to fade on paper, so we checked in with the rangers. The news was not encouraging. The recent rains had swelled the rivers. Because it was still early, no taxi or bus had yet arrived to verify passability. Jim and I listened to the news. Because of his hunting experience in wildernesses, Jim felt confident he could cross the swollen creeks and rivers. The attendants nodded their encouragement and bid us farewell with hugs and handshakes. Within their well wishes, I remembered their parting remark, "First you'll hit the potholes and then there are eight to twelve creeks and rivers to cross. The first crossing is steep, so make sure you make a good run to get out."

For the next half hour, Jim drove our little 4x4 down a mud road filled with potholes so deep they could have swallowed our tires. At times there was no road at all, only a remnant of its edge to ride on. Other times, the holes were as wide as the road and three times the length of the car. I gasped each time we approached one. Finally, Jim asked me to look for birds and tell him what wildlife he was missing. I spotted king vultures, white ibises, roseate spoonbills, parrots, and of course monkeys, and with each bump, I tried not to look at the road. Suddenly the road turned smooth and made for a less tense drive, but that was to change very soon.

The first river crossing came quickly. We were behind a taxi and followed his lead. The next crossing was so severe that I couldn't help crying, "Oh, shit!"

Jim silenced me with a warning look. I realized he needed to hear words of confidence, not my frightful expletives. We watched as the car ahead disappeared from the bank down the dip into the river. The distance to the other side was short, the water level higher than it appeared, the embankment steeper than perceived. I had rolled my window up, but Jim's remained open. Water crested over our hood and splashed inside the window. Jim concentrated on his driving. He suppressed the urge to gun the motor, which would have flooded the engine, and pushed the accelerator with steady pressure. Despite the sputters and coughs, we made it up the bank to the other side. Neither of us said a word.

I know now why the map showed the road to Carate as a dotted line. The space between each line was a pothole, creek, or river crossing. Real roads continue without breaks. The road to Carate wasn't a road, but a series of holes united by mud and asphalt.

The next few river crossings were uneventful, lulling us back to feeling confident about proceeding. Then Jim made the mistake of asking a local taxi driver his opinion of the roads ahead and if he thought that we would make it across the river. He advised us to turn back. Shaken but undeterred, we forged ahead to another large crossing. Jim walked through the river to determine the depth and strength of the water, and to see if there were submerged rocks in our path. While he explored, I brushed off the cobwebs from my Spanish speaking days and asked the property owner, who was relaxing on the porch of his small wooden hut, his opinion.

With a look of compassion, he told me we could cross the river using the path his horse followed. Jim and I warily followed him back into the woods to another opening further up the river. His horse nonchalantly nibbled at the grass. Jim surveyed the opening. To cross here put us in shallower water, but a hundred yards away from the road. After witnessing a motorcyclist with a chainsaw tied to his back seat cross the river from the shallower spot, Jim and I hopped back in our car and followed suit.

As our car glided down toward the river, I kept my mouth shut and my eyes on the bank ahead. Jim steered the car, judging the current's pull, until we were safe on the other side. I glanced back at the property owner. He waved his goodbyes and settled back in his post on the porch. From this point on, I thought for sure the worst was behind us. Then I mentally counted, and I hadn't arrived at the number twelve.

Without the encouragement from another set of strangers, Jim and I would have turned back. The last of the crossings was a double one. The road ended, the river started, a narrow sandbar began, and then the river rushed forward. At this point the width of the river was a hundred and fifty-feet, with many channels. I watched as Jim lifted his pants up over his knees and waded across. I saw the swift current flowing on the other side of the sandbar. Jim returned to the car and stated that this was the end of the line. We would have to wait for the river to recede, or go back. I paced back and forth, knowing that when Jim said no way, he meant it. Then from the other side of the river, we watched as a large black truck easily maneuvered across. I waved the guys down and asked their opinion, *"Crees que podemos cruzar el rio con nuestro 4x4?"* (Do you think we can cross the river with our small 4x4?) The trio nodded yes, and added that they had seen us cross the hardest spots, and this part should be a piece of cake.

Jim remained unconvinced. The men dismounted from their truck. They told us to go for it, and if by chance we got stuck, they would rescue us. Jim relented, and off we went. The first part of the crossing was simple, but as we drove over the sandbar into a deeper and swifter channel, I could already feel the pull of the river's current. Jim's eyes had lost their blue twinkle; his cheeks were tight in concentration, and his hands gripped the steering wheel. Miraculously the motor and tires countered the current's pull, and in minutes we were across, safe on dry land. We heard a congratulatory toot from our Costa Rican angels. Jim honked back, and off we went to the end of the dotted-line road.

After two hours we stumbled out of the 4x4, stiff from tensing our muscles at each pothole and large crossing. Sighing with relief, we approached the wooden building where a crusty, bearded gringo sat on a rocking chair. This was Glen, the guardian of our car for the next four nights while we were at the tented lodge. In a flurry of talk, he hurried us off for the walk along the beach to our destination. Our luggage remained with him until the horse and cart could retrieve it at low tide. With the tide rising quickly, we figured we had about an hour before the beach disappeared.

Jim split our wine stash between our backpacks.

Loaded down with other essentials, we headed out toward the sun and sand. I thought our walk on the beach would be an easy stroll, until we came upon another river to ford. Swelled with the last two days of rain and the incoming tide, the river rushed at us. I looked at Jim to verify our approach, and he smiled and extended his arm. Hand-holding wouldn't do. Instead, Jim placed his hand above my wrist, and I did the same on his arm. Locked together, we supported one another and battled the current. While the water came up to Jim's thighs, it came up to my waist. The slippery rocks made poor steppingstones, but the water cleansed and cooled the sweat from our bodies. We trekked along the beach for what seemed miles, until we spotted on the very last stopping post a sign that read, "Welcome to La Leona Lodge."

Adrian, the owner of the lodge, stood high above the beach waving us up the wooden steps, ready to take us to our tent. Glen had radioed him from his rocking-chair post that we were on our way. To calm our frazzled nerves, Adrian made us piña coladas. We sat at the bar, unable to move, enjoying the salt spray from the Pacific Ocean as a torrential downpour swept over the lodge. We were fortunate to have arrived early. The other guests and the horse cart slogged through the rain in the dark.

Our quarters merged the rustic with the elegant, simultaneously inside and outside. The bamboo walls of the bathroom and shower attached at the back of the platform tent. A coconut shell formed the shower-head. From our tent, we watched pelicans swoosh down along the waves, synchronizing their plunges for fish. We listened to howler monkeys, scarlet macaws, the waves, and the rain.

That first night, the treacherous drive still clung to us. We watched the rain and could only imagine the swelled rivers on our return. Haunted by the thought of a much worse return, Jim drank more than his share of piña coladas and red wine. He even promised the spirit world that if the rain ceased and if the rivers receded, he would gladly turn vegetarian as to further reduce impact on the land. By morning the sun rose with a spectacular orange glow, and the preceding day was forgotten.

Hikes into the Parque Nacional Corcovado revealed a three-toed sloth entwined upside down on a tree branch, families of white-faced capuchin monkeys, spider monkeys, squirrel monkeys, anteaters, and a family of agoutis, which looked like short–eared chestnut-brown rabbits. A group of coatimundis with thick bushy tails and pointed noses raided our tent, rifling through our bags in search of food. One night we slept up in Monkey Camp, where the tents were nestled high in the forest canopy. Small black and green poison-dart frogs hid inside tree crevices. Our evening entertainment was watching a mother and father squirrel monkey with their small babies swing through the branches above, aided only by their long, narrow tails. Hand over hand they traveled, loving parents bringing their half dozen children safely across the forest.

On the day of our return, the sun heated our backs and the pelicans played just off shore. We walked along the beach unencumbered, as the horse and cart carried our luggage and packs. The low tide lapped the beach. The rivers shriveled to a trickle. Our past nightmare of driving through the dotted lines of twelve creeks and rivers felt imagined, though the huge potholes, now empty of water, reminded us of our breathtaking adventure. Jim searched the horizon for birds and thought of our freezer, back home, stocked with elk meat from hunting trips. I smiled at his dilemma, thankful for the spirits who kept us safe.

Continental Divide

This three-week journey across the United States triggered thoughts for my third novel Founding Stones. *The cultural landscape, geology, and choices we make along the way define our conceptions of the world.*

I am a voyeur, not a peeping-tom with improper intent, but a traveler who views the world without needing to know the minute details, the why of everything. I watch through windows, not hiding my excitement, the sensuality of what I see. My husband Jim is of another breed, a biologist who sees the world and constantly asks questions to discern what makes it tick. He looks for meaning through the eyes of science.

We're headed across the northern part of the United States, from Western Washington over the Cascades, through Eastern Washington, across the Rockies and then the Great Plains to Duluth, Minnesota. Our mission in Duluth has nothing to do with the western shore of the largest lake in the world, Lake Superior, home of the Masabi Range of iron ore. It just happens to be the town chosen for an international wetlands conference Jim is attending, the meeting place of bogs to the north and prairie potholes to the south and west.

As we start the journey, he informs me in his excited voice, "This is the top of three watersheds, the Hudson Bay, the Gulf of Mexico, and the Atlantic Ocean." I nod, placing a stack of road maps along the glove box that divides our seats.

Traveling in a VW pop-top camper van from Washington State to Minnesota is the antidote to my geography lessons of long ago. Depth and understanding come slowly with each mile from the Columbia River. No one had ever mentioned the Clarke-Fork River or the Yellowstone River in my geography and history lessons, yet they take us across Montana and snake back and forth into Wyoming. Crossing the Continental Divide means leaving the Rockies behind and letting the Missouri River begin its flow to the Mississippi River.

Jim poses the question, "Which of these two rivers is larger, the Missouri or the Mississippi?"

My lessons in geography told me the Mississippi, but as we travel, the Missouri looms large. Remembering our studies of the Louisiana Purchase, we wonder if the naming of the main stem of the rivers had more to do with the politics and the economy of that time period than the real driver of the habitat—spring rains flowing into the flood plain and through New Orleans.

The VW speeds up and over into Montana and the city of Missoula, a college town celebrating graduations and hosting a convention for Jehovah's Witnesses, on the Friday night just before Memorial Day. Each hotel answers our query for a room with a shake of the head, a raising of their hands, and a look that says, "No rooms available at this inn."

Jim, weary from driving twelve hours, insists we will find a campsite before dark. With his assurances, we head into the valleys where roads for mining silver and lead bring us to smaller towns. Veering just off Highway 94, we abandon the more touristy routes and search for a camping site. The long days give us light, but as the sun sets, we take back roads to find a hidden spot, and in my tired opinion, any spot. Whenever I notice a pull-out, a turnaround edge, or even an imprint of space, I muster up an unconvincing plea, "We could pull off here, camp, and be gone before anyone would notice."

Jim, now on a mission, keeps driving, until miraculously the turns take us to a campground with an empty site. Now in the Missouri watershed, we pop our van top and that of a bottle of wine, and celebrate our first night out.

∞

Up before the sun, we hike along Bear Creek trail, deeper into the woods, till we cross a small bridge where water makes its way from the hills above. Jim brews a pot of French Press coffee, a necessary indulgence. Packed, we make our way out, past the nudges of spaces, fishing pullouts where a few cars parked for the night, campers less patient than us. The parting gift, a herd of Rocky Mountain sheep grazing along the winding road, ignores us as we drive back to the highway.

We breakfast in Philipsburg, a town of only one open café. Our waitress, at least six inches shorter than my five feet, rules the café with her boisterous and confident greetings; she bounces from table to table. I look atop her head for rubies and sapphires, a crown of sorts, as Phillipsburg is famed for these stones.

Gems, the lure of success, prepare us for the hills of copper in Anaconda and the forever changing landscape where the veins of time, majestic fortresses of colored minerals, press together and rise up the valley hillside. Here is where the confusion of water begins. Jim talks of the Columbia River and the Snake River as they meld. To me they disappear, converge, and I can no longer find the discerning line. Jim's excitement progresses, his fingers pointing as he refers to map after map. He wants to find the exact spot where we lose our familiar watershed waterways and wetlands.

I stare out the window, watching the shifting of rivers, the burned trees like whiskers poking up in a crewcut of hills, the stubble of past forest fires, the exposed skin of the earth, until we dip south into the northwest tip of Wyoming—the headwaters of the Yellowstone River.

We stretch our legs at Yellowstone National Park, where the wetlands boil. Old Faithful, a geyser spewing hot steam, draws crowds of tourists. Lines of onlookers weave along paths, and we blend among them, awed by the impressive burping of sulfur, the bubbling of gases from deep within the earth, all centered in this vast area. My legs, no longer cramped in the van, feel the rise of steps, the letting go of tightness, but the crush of beings surrounding each site stifles my peace. I feel the crowds as walls; I'm claustrophobic. All of us selfishly vie for a place to see the timed explosion of Old Faithful, the countdown and impatient tick of minutes. Secretly Old Faithful's tardy gurgles pleases me, the reminder that cycles are cycles and that nature is unpredictable. The triumphant spew, ten minutes late, receives healthy applause, and Old Faithful tweets an extra fountain for an encore.

Jim and I seek areas less crowed, sites less advertised but still impressive, small pots of gases and mud, colored blue and yellow by algae, with flowers hiding inside. I see thoughts creep along Jim's forehead, and with his tongue firmly in cheek, he asks, "I wonder why temperature isn't in the federal guidance manual for wetlands." Work and pleasure mix in his brain, a curse and an opportunity to learn.

Unsure of where to camp, we find the Fishing Bridge R.V. Park Area, with warnings from the camp host, "Keep your Yeti cooler inside your van, your pop-top sealed—a mother grizzly just booted out its three-month-old cub. The cub was spotted here yesterday."

So much for my peeing outside in the middle of the night. I squelch nature's call by sleeping on my side, listening for the scrounging paws of a hungry cub.

∞

Early morning mist hangs over Yellowstone Falls, but the roar of water cascading down the canyon, with the sun casting shadows, draws us into the edges. The crack of time, the working of energy, the power and beauty stand before us. As insignificant viewers, we witness nature's supremacy. The Grand Canyon of the Yellowstone River, the result of a huge volcanic eruption 640,000 years ago, left a giant caldera that filled with lava, ready for the river's role in exposing time. The sun casts light on the lower falls, onto multi-hued rocks, yellows and oranges: rainbow rocks of geology.

Jim names the rock and the process, "Sulfide and carbon dioxide alter the rhyolite. That's why the stones are yellow."

I smile, happy for the information, but only able to absorb the rays of color, the grandiose display of mist, the product of years of weathering.

Climbing upward to 8000 feet, we leave the park through the Silver Gate with snow piled on the sides of the road and flakes tumbling toward us, a spring snowstorm. We breakfast in Cooke City at an oasis of simple food, fireplace crackling and an old piano playing. Hearty town folk come and go as we warm ourselves by the fire, eat our English muffin egg sandwiches, and hold our hot coffee mugs.

From here the terrain changes dramatically. If I thought Yellowstone National Park was impressive, the morphing of landscape now redefines my perceptions. The park includes both Montana and Wyoming, and now we slip back into Montana, where coal dominates the economy and sandstone and mudstone the landscape. We shift from the Rocky Mountains to the Great Plains. Jim notes the floodplains and backwater wetlands as we come to Pompey's Pillar, a massive sandstone base on the banks of the Yellowstone River—a monument famous for Captain William Clark's signature, graffiti that marks Lewis and Clark travels. I sense the irony of the signs and cameras placed to admonish tourists and implore them to refrain from carving the stone with their own initials. Oh, how we as a people want to mark our territory, name our spot, declare our existence.

Railroad tracks carrying extended freight trains of coal dip in and out of sight as we head to Glendive, Montana. And here is where the weather becomes a verb, visually changing before our eyes. Now in the Great Plains, the skyscape opens and the clouds mark what is to come.

Our drive to Glendive races the lightning and thunder. Dark thunder clouds spread out around us, rain waves pointing the way of the storm. More than once the pellets of rain obscure the road, and the downpour accumulates in pools of water making the highway a river. Jim feigns nonchalance, but I note how he switches the windshield-wipers to high, how he hugs the edge of the two-lane highway. Straight roads, no visibility, and zigzagged bolts of light punctuate the blue-black sky. With our arrival in Glendive, the rain dissipates and the dark clouds float off to the north. We know that we are lucky, as other visitors show evidence of the storm on the hoods of their cars, pockmarks from golf-sized hail.

The town, with a population the size of a small-town high school, boasts two hotels, with four in construction. Signs say that Glendive lies within a prehistoric sea and the newly-discovered coal and natural gas sites from the Bakken Shale Formation. This is black gold. Drilling crews, one truck after another, drive the pot-holed roads. Even though the shale formation is centered in North Dakota, the real boom in Williston has spilled out to these towns. I see the past in the present, the frenzy of the gold rush, the hunger to make good without understanding the consequences. Lined along the highway, machines used for drilling outnumber the multitude of John Deere tractors. Pumps sit adjacent to the farmed fields, lone metal structures moving silently up and down on pads of concrete, surrounded by corn and wheat fields, with a pyre flame for excess gases.

Mining and fracking touch everyone; the issue isn't political, but one of common sense. We heed this as a gentle warning from the manager of the hotel, the daughter of an engineer who makes his living maintaining drilling equipment. "Remain neutral, be nonjudgmental visitors." As we eat at the recommended diner, everyone wears the grime of a long day at work. Jim devours his slab of beef. I eat their version of stir-fry vegetables. Our conversation veers away from the obvious. Consequences for the groundwater and surface water are far from the laborer's radar screen. We understand this to be a town of pragmatists. The new discovery buried within the earth creates a livelihood and guarantees survival.

Glendive's fame for buried treasures, to Jim's delight, includes dinosaurs. Survival for the dinosaurs ended around the Cretaceous period, and the Makoshika State Park just out of town has us hiking and hunting fossils in the hills where the first Tyrannosaurus rex fossil was found. Roaming for me is not easy, as the badlands are steep and rugged, oozing mud from the recent thunderstorms. With binoculars on my shoulder, a camera around my neck, and a walking stick for balance, I slide on every incline until finally my shoes suck in the mud and my left hand and walking stick hold me in too precarious a position. Mud baths, I'm told, are great for the skin. I use the edges of rocks to pry off the ancestral goo, and Jim hands me a wet cloth to wipe my hands. We leave, satisfied that nature has in its wisdom created steppingstones of magnificent blocks as resting stones for the dinosaurs.

On our way out of Glendive we stop at the local fish hotspot, the "intake" for agriculture on the Yellowstone River, to discover in these badlands a freshwater fish, mammoth in ugliness and beauty. The paddlefish, waiting to gain energy for its jump up the diversion dam, is the local favorite. Families stake their spot early in the day. We watch fisher folk measure and weigh, and harvest the roe to make caviar. Most of the locals eat the fish, preferably before it grows to maturity, claiming the smaller, the tastier. While I snap pictures of the long paddle snout, stick my nose in roe, and pose with just the two-foot head and snout, Jim studies the river and talks with the fishers. He learns that thirty percent of the proceeds from the caviar go to the Montana Fish, Wildlife, and Parks program to fund paddlefish research. Nice returns for these ancient fish with no scales.

From the intake we head back into the prairie through the badlands dipping back into Wyoming. Turkey vultures fly over—an omen of sorts. This, their home, is as rugged as the mountain spikes rising up above the flat plains. I sense the vastness, the endless rising and falling of peaks and valleys. Banded colors of eroded rock extend on a horizontal plane as if the sun strikes lines through the strata. Loneliness and beauty: a place of awe, respect, and danger. The badlands render another surprise off the road south of Wibaux near Ekalaka: large sandstone rocks, dubbed Medicine Rocks by the Native Americans, remnants of an ancient sea. I first judge the name a tourist trick to entice the crowds, something to draw us in. I'm wrong. Here, the towering ochre and red sandstone monuments hold the spirits, creating—*inya-oka-laka*—rocks with holes, arches and artistic sculptures that heal with energy of long ago. I feel more than at Yellowstone, or the stomping ground of the dinosaurs, the serene yet powerful work of time.

After roaming amongst the Medicine Rocks, we head farther south into Wyoming. The big sky and straight roads continue on and on. Jim speaks his thoughts out loud, tells me how the badlands earned their formations. I haven't asked, but I know it helps him understand. "The steep slopes are made of soft clay and silt from the ancient sea and capped with sand. Rivulets and rills run through the slopes, and over time the cutting action creates the steppingstones."

I let the words—rivulets, rills, and run—roll off my tongue, feeling the roll of our VW taking us through time.

∞

When we arrive in the Belle Fourche river valley, I gasp in disbelief at a rising stone pillar. Jim surprises me with a place not on my bucket list, Devil's Tower. Jim has been here before, and he watches my eyes as I take in the rise of thousands of feet. This was the first national monument declared by President Theodore Roosevelt, but to the Native Americans, who worshiped the tower, it was the spirits rising, bears clawing in a showdown of native legend. The geological explanation is equally dramatic—magma plug stuck in a volcano, worn away through time, so that the volcano disappeared, exposing the tower. We camp near it, awestruck by the seven-sided basalt columns and the boulder-size scree.

After our first cup of coffee, we return to hike in the scree. It takes us an hour to circle the tower. The large crumbling of the stone reminds that sometime in the future, other generations will see only remnants, that the weathering away will eventually erode the magma plug, and the past will not be anyone's present.

As we drive on to Mt. Rushmore, two coal trains pass along separate tracks. This is an optical illusion, fast flashes splintering in two directions at once. Sun spashes off metal as their hundred cars rush along in opposite directions—modern man's artistic mark. Mt. Rushmore, man-made carving, was more a homage, a larger than life memorial to our famous presidents. I feel the same as I had at Yellowstone National Park, an obligation to see something famous. The best I can do is wink at my namesake, Abraham Lincoln, pleased at his inclusion.

∞

Heading back to what we dub the good land of the badlands, north to South Dakota, we take an exit different from our impressive entrance of four-lane roads. Our exit takes us on three 360-degree roundabouts, onto bridges shored up with wood pilings, and one-lane tunnels going in two directions. Straight, dusty gravel roads, more thunderstorms, a tornado, and hail, and hours of driving bring us to the Sage Creek Campsite—a spot that combines the elements of the Great Plains, badlands, grasslands, and prairie pot-holes.

Here we find posts surrounding sand, reminiscent of wagon trains where the settlers huddled together in a circle. We park our van above the tents that line the sandy area, not far from a horse trailer. The grassy area is covered in cracked mud and buffalo pies. Across a road and field, a herd of wild buffalo graze. With thunder clouds above us, we cross our fingers that the rains will not drench the ground. That the mud will remain solidified, that our van doesn't sink into the ancient mud-goo. That night we sleep with our Yeti cooler outside, our pop-top open wide. While Jim snores beside me, I count after each lightning strike, never getting past five before the thunder rolls. I smell the rains, the grass, and the musty scent of buffalo.

In the morning Mother Nature calls us awake even before the rising sun. Our full bladders can't wait for relief. Jim climbs down from our bed and I follow. We step out onto moist grass to three bull buffalo greeting us by our door with the prehistoric sounds of munching, wide heads bowed in concentration, ignoring us but aware. The poster at the campsite warned of signs of agitation: the lifting of the tail, the stare down, the rolling on the ground. We venture out with cameras, slowly judging the tension. When one of the buffalo begins to rock its mammoth head from side to side, we slip back inside. But the tail remains down, and the stare never comes. As the buffalo move on, they roll on the grass, leaving brown oily spots with pockets of long strands of hair in the form of dreadlocks. This is their shedding season, their version of a haircut. Half hairy, half skinned, the male buffalo saunter off with Jim following to collect their dreads.

The rain has only moistened the ground, and we drive off without getting stuck in the ancestral ooze. Five miles down the road we spot black dots peppering the grassy fields. Binoculars in hand, we watch a herd of fifty-some female buffalo graze with their newly-born calves. Our parting memory is the view of the prairie, flat before the spikes of the badlands, where light brown prairie dogs bob up and down from their underground holes. I stifle a laugh and stare in amusement. Standing on two feet, their arms curled in anticipation, they ask the question, "What? What is so funny?"

∞

The landscape morphs as we head to our ultimate destination, Duluth, Minnesota, for Jim's wetlands conference. With tornado warnings and more thunderstorms blowing in from the south, we decide to drive on a more northerly road and transfer our sightseeing to Interstate 90. Green grass is everywhere, dancing with the breezes. Jim cranes his head at every turn to see birds, antelope, and the land. His banter is worth listening to, and as I watch the terrain change, he blurts out the obvious but profound statement, "The earth is not homogenous, and neither are people."

True, how can we expect to see the world the same way when the elements change on us? How can we make rules to govern every situation when we as a people aren't homogenous? Hidden in Jim's statement is the question of how our government inherently works to eliminate our differences, blending one landscape into another, and all cultures into its own.

I talk with a woman who runs a museum during the summer months. She tells us about her 8000 acres of grassland and how she rounds up her cattle in a snowstorm. Survival isn't a choice. Her herds believe in her, and she alone saves them. She smiles, telling us how she now enjoys her cell phone. "I feel safer if I run into trouble on my four-wheeler. That is, if I can get reception."

I have no idea how to live in a world of large acreages of grasses, or the harsh winters of never-ending snow. Self-reliance and working with the elements isn't the same for those living in cities. Climate, terrain, and the vast distances between homes and towns change an individual.

In Minnesota we enter an area of bogs and lakes. Wetlands, the prairie pot-holes of isolated waters from North Dakota, disappear, overpowered by the largest area of lakes in the world. Again, green is everywhere. I listen to the plunk of the roads, a rhythmic sound as we bounce on notches where the cold of winter and hot of summer create a buckle. Jim can almost see the expansion and contraction, just like what causes scree. In between the farmlands of thousands of acres, railroad tracks zigzag through the fields to towns far away, iron mines, and cities; the Boundary Waters take precedence. The Great Lakes shape the people just as the desolation of the Badlands does; the harsh winters of the prairies establish self-reliance. Here the towns remain small, everyone drives a pickup truck trailing a boat, and fishing is what you do. We stay at a resort along a large lake just outside of Canada. The restaurant is packed with locals, here more for the beauty than the food. They come in their boats, share fish stories, and eat Walleye.

I am overcome by the city of Duluth, its adaption to industry and its vibrancy as a welcoming larger city. Lake Superior rules life. On its shores, cold winds blow despite the sun. I see the mixture of cultures, the domination of the iron industry—railroad tracks for freight only, the work of art in a bridge that opens to allow the vast ships carrying coal, iron, and other mined products to cities and towns across our country. Before Jim's conference we visit an iron pit, witness the making of round pellets the size of peas that will be used to make steel. Truck after truck carries the pellets to the railroads.

While Jim learns about canary-grass research in the Ukraine and the problems in Sri Lanka with maintaining wetland habitats, I try to put thoughts together. I see our infrastructure, the byways, the highways, railroads, and shipping routes, connected to what is inside our great earth. I see each river connected, each mountain range separated by ancient seas. We live in a world that compresses time, minerals, and dinosaurs, and extracts raw material to create steel for bridges, harvesting crops from farms and even farming fish. As we change this landscape, we affect the place where we live—curse or improvement? I'm struck by the fact that coal comes from peat, compressed in our precious wetlands. I see cycles of life.

Time, as my husband Jim states, is life. I value it all. I want the scablands, the badlands, and the wetlands to be treated with respect—our Goodland.

Dung Beetle

Kenya and Tanzania are only two countries within the vast continent of Africa. Expansive geography, animals, tribal rivalry, and culture are illuminated through the eyes of this emblematic insect.

If my ramblings appear erratic, blame this on the rough roads of time. Even as I write, three days after my month-long journey into Kenya and Tanzania, my dreams bump along rutted paths. The image of a dung beetle whispers in my unconscious brain. I see the determined roll of cattle dung into a ball ten times the beetle's size for the purpose of securing the future of beetle eggs. A mud puddle becomes a vast ocean, a treacherous crossing of life and death.

I toss and turn, mistaking my bed covers for the red robes of the Maasai Tribe. *Karibu!!!* Welcome into the world of cattle tending. Mud dung walls and straw roofs, a windowless room called home. Circular patterns of families cooking with bundled sticks. Huts surround livestock. Women cook, milk the cows, gather firewood, weave baskets, bead ceremonial necklaces, and tend to the children. I smell smoke. My bare feet ooze with the mud of puddle paths, my day decided by my ancestors.

Nadifunja. I am learning Swahili, the official language of East Africa. Each tribe speaks its own tongue. Forty-two tribes in Kenya, one hundred and twenty tribes in Tanzania, yet all are bound by Swahili. Education means change. I practice greetings— *jambo*, hello, and *asante sana*, thank you very much. Those in school also learn English, a remnant of the British holdings. Language symbolizes a step into the future. Chagrined that I know only English and speak sparse Spanish, I ponder the American emphasis on assimilation. Africans take on old rhythms and hear them in each language—the tapping of sticks that prod cattle along and the chants of women as they perform ceremonial dances. My feet stomp, my hips sway. I watch men jumping, warriors rising high to see the game.

Never far from any city or road, wild animals roam. Zebra, gazelle, giraffe, ostrich, and the dotted outline of umbrella acacia trees form the background of the countryside. Both Kenya and Tanzania preserve their wildlife with national parks surrounded by buffers. The Maasai roam freely. In their mind this is their right, their destiny, their essence. Transplanted outside of the national parks, they live on reserves and travel through countries, bound not by nationality but by the roaming of their cattle.

Jumping warriors protect their cattle from lions, leopards, and hyenas. Bound by tribal traditions, the boys and men walk along the savannah, the hills, into any and all areas. Warriors, they defend the right to herd cattle and measure their wealth by the number of livestock they own. Without other currency, without other food, the Maasai drink the blood of the cattle, mixing it with milk. Remnants of polygamy remain as an old legacy for survival. Wealthy elders with many cows need their cows milked, which means many wives.

Now the elders embrace change, more schools inside the hutted villages. They have left behind female genital mutilation in favor of health. Warriors still must prove themselves by the ritual of late male circumcision. To flinch brings shame, so boys practice pain tolerance with burns on their skin. Livestock currency is exchanged for the currency of British shillings—a trade for clean water, health. Survival of the fittest includes economics. Beaded wedding necklaces and ebony talking sticks are sold to the tourist market.

Mt. Kilimanjaro looms large along the border between Kenya and Tanzania. The highest mountain in Africa contains the coveted ebony that the Maasai use for their talking sticks. Civilized in ways of communicating, the elders never point when they speak. A talking stick, carved and polished, rich with the black of ebony, includes a long handle topped off with a knob. This knob paves the way of talking. I'm reminded of the muted colors of the giraffe, long necked elegance, peering over the greens of tall trees. The slant of their necks, pointers in the distance, informs the landscape. Giraffes neck to show their power. Warriors in their own way, the males wrap their necks with forceful blows. To neck is to fight, but not to hurt. The giraffe, like the Maasai warrior, seeks only a mate.

I dream in color, the colors of Africa: green, yellow, red, black, white. Nesting birds hang their nests, woven with strands of green fronds and straw, upside down. Metallic blue, lemon yellow feathers—nothing in Africa mutes the intensity of life. The Serengeti pulses with fervor. I imagine myself a wildebeest on the grand migration. Following the rains from the Mara, crossing the river to the savannah, hundreds of thousands run, guided by the seeing eyes of the zebra, to the green grassy lands. Wildebeest instinct propels my legs hundreds of miles, for the food and place to birth. I hold my belly, which carries a child. The rains trigger the flight and also trigger the wait. If the land is lacking in food, nature holds the birth. Rituals, traditions, patterns mix with the migration. Crocodiles know I am on my way, waiting along the river shores, and lions look for the weak babies, the ones that don't run fast enough, that stumble for longer than a few minutes to find their legs. Bones, left for the picking, decorate the Serengeti plains.

Other bones creak into my dreams. Stranded in the Serengeti, our jeep sinks farther into the muck of the rutted roads. I spot the bones of an elephant, skin still intact, but holes remain where tusks belong. Poachers are the marketers of ivory. Vultures soar overhead, flies swarm. I imagine my bones mingling with those in Olduvai gorge, bones so old they precede that of Homo sapiens. Ancient bones of time rattle the land.

My hand touches that of a small child from the Iraqwi fishing village. The elders stare with closed lips, the children dance and smile. Here, the first school started in 2009. The elders speak only their tribal tongue. I clasp the innocence and joy of this child's hand. I hear the ancient chants of the women from the Maasai tribe. My feet move with toes pointed forward, bones from the genetic legacy of the Olduvai. I dream of the dung beetle rolling along.

Book Group Questions

1. What themes permeate this collection? What themes run through your own life?

2. If you were given a chance to highlight a moment in time, which moment would you show?

3. Humor and pain are two sides of the same coin. How do these stories reflect that?

4. Perspective is everything. Take one of the selections from this book and view it through different lenses. Find the opposite viewpoint and see where that takes you.

5. Travel is a metaphor for life. We talk of other cultures, their history and customs. Is there commonality between all people, young and old? (Strengths, weaknesses)

6. What does your sock drawer look like? Do you have a junk drawer? How do you pack a suitcase? Have any of these habits changed over time?

About The Author

Abbe Rolnick grew up in the suburbs of Baltimore, Maryland. Her first major cultural jolt occurred at age 15 when her family moved to Miami Beach, Florida, where history came alive with her exposure to the Cuban culture and inspired her to write about her observations. At Boston University she met her first husband, a native of Puerto Rico. Her first novel, **RIVER OF ANGELS**, stems from her experiences while living in Puerto Rico and owning an independent bookstore. Later, back Stateside, she was one of the first employees at now-famous Village Books in Bellingham, WA. She now owns a healthy foods cafe.

COLOR OF LIES, her second novel, brings the reader to the Pacific Northwest where she now resides with her husband on twenty acres in Skagit Valley, Washington. Here she blends stories from island life with characters in Skagit Valley.

Her next novel, **FOUNDING STONES**, will be the third in the series, continuing the stories of characters from the two previous novels, introducing new themes that connect Skagit Valley to the larger world.

Abbe's short stories and travel pieces have appeared in several magazines. "Swinging Doors" won honorary mention in a *Writer's Digest* contest. Her recent experiences with her husband's journey through multiple myeloma inspired **COCOON OF CANCER: AN INVITATION TO LOVE DEEPLY.**

CPSIA information can be obtained
at www.ICGtesting.com
Printed in the USA
FSOW01n0016210616
21799FS